AFRICAN WRITERS SERIES

Founding editor · Chinua Achebe

Keys to Signs

Novels are unmarked
*Short Stories
†Poetry
‡Plays
§Autobiography or Biography

AFRICAN WRITERS SERIES

163

Warrior King

Warrior King

Sahle Sellassie

HEINEMANN

LONDON · NAIROBI · IBADAN · LUSAKA

Heinemann Educational Books Ltd
48 Charles Street, London WıX 8AH
P.M.B. 5205, Ibadan · P.O. Box 45314, Nairobi
P.O. Box 3966, Lusaka

EDINBURGH MELBOURNE TORONTO AUCKLAND SINGAPORE
HONG KONG KUALA LUMPUR NEW DELHI

ISBN 0 435 90163 X

Printed in Great Britain by
Richard Clay (The Chaucer Press), Ltd.,
Bungay, Suffolk

Contents

I

The Old Man's Tale

For weeks on end the people of Quara district talked of nothing but Kassa Hailu and his followers, who had dared to attack the district governor and finally to chase him out to Gondar, the capital of the disintegrated empire. Those who were familiar with the name 'Kassa' talked about him with sheer admiration while others, especially women who confined themselves to home affairs, ignorant of what was going on around them, craved to know who this man Kassa was and what secret power he possessed that hypnotised the youth of the district, and made them creep after him. Many a father tried to explain to his son the dangers of going out to the bush to join the rebels headed by Kassa; many a mother wept to see her son rush off to the jungle. But all was in vain. The young ones went, while the old ones stayed at home to tell tales.

'Who is he? Who is this man called Kassa?' a woman asked. She was the mother of a young man who was preparing to join the rebels.

'Kassa? You don't know Kassa?' The father of the young man was surprised by his wife's ignorance.

'No, I never heard of him until today.'

'The entire district of Quara has been talking about him the last few weeks, and you tell me you have never heard of him until today?'

'I swear in the name of St Michael that I have never heard of Kassa until today, father of Gebreye, and I want to know who he is.'

'He is the son of Hailu, Hailu Wolde-Giorgis.'

'And who is Hailu? Who is Wolde-Giorgis?' None of the names meant anything to her.

'You have such a poor memory, Aberash! Don't you recall an incident which I admit took place a very long time ago – in fact, twenty-five years ago – an incident everybody in our village talked about for months, an incident in which were involved Dejach Maru, the governor of Dembia district, and Hailu Wolde-Giorgis? Don't you remember how Dejach Maru, the governor of Dembia, after seeing Hailu's wife dancing during the epiphany festival, became almost mad about her, and how the entire population of Quara and Dembia reacted to it?'

'Ye-e-e-e-s,' Aberash said hesitantly, the tip of her finger between her teeth, her eyebrows knitted in thought. Then, her mind suddenly flooded by remembrance, she cried out, 'Oh, yes! That wretched business! Why, I do remember it now.'

'You do?'

'Yes, I remember everything distinctly. It was said that the governor proposed to pay five hundred Maria Theresa dollars to the poor husband if he would agree to divorce his wife. And how shocking that was to all decent people in our area!'

'Right, right,' Mulatu confirmed, happy that his wife's memory was not dead, after all. 'And perhaps you recall too that Hailu sent back a message to Maru telling him that he wouldn't accept even five thousand dollars, let alone five hundred, that his wife was not an article for sale, and that he did not expect such an insult from him or from anyone else. Poor as he was, he must have been tempted a great deal to divorce his wife for such a large sum. But he was a proud and noble

2

man at heart, that Hailu! May God bless his soul.' Mulatu coughed.

'But I don't recall how the matter ended up.'

'You don't? Well, what does a powerful man like Maru do when he wants something, and that something cannot be had by persuasion? I mean when it cannot be had in a friendly way?'

'I suppose he uses force.'

'Precisely,' Mulatu cried out. 'That's precisely what Dejach Maru did. He had Hailu's wife kidnapped.'

'And is that the way it ended?'

'No, no. It did not end at that. Hailu, although crushed by poverty, had the heart of a lion. He was the type of man who, they say, never forgets or forgives. And his mind was set on revenge. He borrowed a musket from one of Maru's own followers and made an attempt on his foe's life. Being a bad shot, however, he succeeded only in wounding Maru in the belly. I heard from a close friend of Hailu's that he aimed at Maru's body just below the navel, but instead wounded him just above that part. Then he fled to Gondar disguised in the clothes of a Moslem trader, something like what our neighbour Ibrahim usually wears. In Gondar he had a bell rung, according to our tradition, and sought refuge in one of the forty-four inviolable shrines. Thus he escaped Maru's revenge. It is said that after a few weeks' stay there he left the shrine, married a rather obscure woman from the district of Infraz and lived in the outskirts of the capital. Now Kassa, the rebel leader whose force our Gebreye wants to join, is the son of that Hailu who went on self-exile about twenty-five years ago and lived in Gondar until his death only a year or two later. Is this clear to you now?'

'Yes, it is very clear, father of Gebreye. But tell me everything about this young man called Kassa.'

'It is a long story, Aberash. I am afraid you will be bored by it. Besides, my throat will crack open with dryness if I try to tell you all about him now.'

'Don't worry about my being bored, father of Gebreye. And I will bring you tella to drink so that your throat will not crack up with dryness,' she said, understanding what he wanted. She trotted away to the guada, to return instantly with a jar of the home-made beer and a wancha. She filled the utensil and handed it to her husband after tasting the drink herself as was the custom.

'Well,' Mulatu said, putting down his wancha on the earth floor before him, 'so you want me to tell you everything about Kassa?'

'That's why I am bribing you!'

'All right, all right,' he laughed. 'I would tell you all I know about him even if you didn't bribe me. To begin from the beginning, it is generally believed that Kassa was born after a monk had made a prophecy about him. When he was in his mother's womb – his mother's name was Attetegeb, if it interests you to know that – a holy monk wearing a skull-cap and a cow-hide appeared before the poor woman and said to her: "The fruit in your womb is a son. He shall become one of the greatest rulers that this country has ever produced. But woe to the Church! woe to the people!" And then he disappeared from her sight. He could of course have said that simply to please Attetegeb, who gave him alms. But with whatever motive he uttered those words, the child in Attetegeb's womb indeed turned out to be a son – no other than Kassa himself. Apparently Kassa heard of the prophecy later on in life from his mother and came to believe in it.

'As the story goes, when Hailu died Attetegeb could not bring up the child herself because of her poverty, so she confided him to his powerful uncle Kenfu, who soon confided him in turn to the Mahbere Sellassie convent where our own Gebreye went to school.'

Ato Mulato paused here to have his wancha refilled. He loved tella very much, so much so that he could empty a whole jar by himself at one sitting and still remain sober.

'Go on. Go on,' Aberash urged him, refilling his wancha.

'Well, Kassa stayed in the Mahbere Sellassie convent for quite a few years. Some time after our Gebreye finished with his schooling, an unfortunate thing happened in the Mahbere Sellassie convent which finally caused Kassa to quit it. As the story is told, Maru, angered by numerous foes who were conniving to oust him from his governorship, sacked the Mahbere Sellassie convent. Like the Roman whose name escapes me, but which is written in the Holy Bible, he massacred their innocent children by way of revenge. Kassa, however, escaped the cowardly massacre as if by a miracle and fled here to Quara to stay with his uncle Dejach Kenfu. I suppose you are following me, Aberash?'

'Of course, of course. You said Maru was trying to avenge himself against Hailu by trying to kill his son.'

'Not exactly. You are misinterpreting what I said. What I actually said was that Maru was trying to avenge himself on all those who wanted to oust him from his governorship.'

'That's what I meant. And then you said Kassa came to live with his uncle.'

'Right.' Mulatu cleared his throat and continued: 'Well, Kassa became a popular lad during his stay at Dejach Kenfu's. It is there that I myself met him the first time.'

'You met him?'

'Oh, yes. Although I wouldn't know what he looks like now, he was a very charming boy at that time, the type who promises much, you know. He was agile and graceful in appearance, like the young of a cheetah. He outshined his age-mates in prac-

5

tically everything he did, be it playing gugse, wrestling, running or horse-riding. One day I saw him with my own eyes leap on to a trotting horse without a saddle or rein, with the ease and grace of a cheetah. And Dejach Kenfu loved him like his own sons, in fact more than his own sons who lacked his daring spirit. He took him along with him everywhere he went, to the Chechelo jungle for elephant hunts or to the Sudan border to fight the Turks. The bloody . . .'

Mulatu broke off suddenly as if struck by lightning. His mind flew back to days past to watch the panoramic view of fez-wearing red men engaging in battle against black men wearing lions' manes on their heads; to watch sabres clashing against sabres; huts burning; women and children weeping; vultures hovering around the dead bodies of valiant warriors.

'What is wrong with you, father of Gebreye? Why did you break off?' Aberash asked him, somewhat puzzled.

'I am horrified by what I see, but what you don't, Aberash. I see a bloody war raging along the Sudan border, and amidst it all I see the intestine of my nephew torn out of his belly with a hooked spear. He is in agony. He is dying. He is dead.'

'You seem to be suffering from hallucinations! But is that really the way your nephew died?'

'Yes, in Metema, many, many years ago.'

Mulatu had totally retired from military activities only after an accident that cost him dear. His misfortune began the day he fell off his mule and struck his knee against a stone. He moaned with pain day and night for two solid months following the fall. His knee grew in size every day until it was as big as a pumpkin. It was full of pus and black blood, as was discovered at the end of the two months when a village physician called Amede cut it open with the splinter of a broken green bottle and let the pus and the black blood flow out. He had a respite at last, when the content was out, and slept in peace for the first time in eight weeks. The wound healed, but left Mulatu crippled. And as a result Mulatu was released from any call to war, unlike the other peasants who tilled their land in time of peace and took up their arms in time of war.

'Do you know how the bards used to praise Dejach Kenfu?' Mulatu asked his wife, his mind still brooding over the past.

'I have no idea.'

'They used to sing: "Black was the lance of Kenfu, but it is changing colour. It is getting redder and redder with the blood of the Turks."'

'That sounds good.'

'And you know how his sister wailed upon his death?'

'I get embarrassed when you ask me such questions, father of Gebreye, because you know that I am ignorant of such things.'

'I don't really mean to embarrass you, my dear. It's just my way of saying things.'

'How did Kenfu's sister wail?'

> The great eagle shall fly no more
> From Quara to Metema,
> Now that Kenfu is clipped.

'That's how she wailed.'

'I don't understand that one.'

'I don't blame you for it. Here Kenfu's sister is playing on words. You know that Kenfu is the name of her brother, but it also means "Its wings." And so her dirge runs like this:

> The great eagle shall fly no more
> From Quara to Metema,
> Now that its wings are clipped.

'She is representing Dejach Kenfu as a great eagle. And as an

7

eagle with clipped wings cannot fly, likewise Dejach Kenfu can wage no more war against the Turks because he is dead.'

'I see! His sister must have been a very clever woman, unlike me. But you haven't finished telling me about Kassa.'

'Oh, no, I went off the subject. Where did I break off?'

'You said Kassa followed Dejach Kenfu to the Chechelo jungle for elephant hunts, and to the Sudan border to fight the Turks.'

'That's right. I'm glad you were following the story attentively,' he observed. He took another sip of the tella and went on to say: 'Well, Dejach Kenfu died soon afterwards, and his sons started to fight against each other over the governorship of Quara. That's the type of thing that really makes me feel sick, you know. Since the fall of the empire, that's what has been going on – brother fighting brother, son-in-law fighting father-in-law – well, this country's history has been written in blood and keeps on being written in blood. Until such time as a strong hand reunites the scattered provinces the fight will go on, I tell you. Anyhow, to come back to what I was saying, Kassa sided with the elder brother in the power struggle that followed the death of Dejach Kenfu. But before the outcome of their struggle could be known, Dejach Goshu of Gojam, seeing that the two brothers were weakened by fighting each other, attacked and defeated them both. Kassa, who had fought by the side of Kenfu's sons, soon disappeared, thereby escaping Goshu's punishment. No one knew his whereabouts for a whole month. But then it was discovered that he had hidden in a peasant's hut for some time and that afterwards he had left for the western border to lead a band of highway robbers. It is said that he had a hard time living in the jungle as a highway robber. He and his band lived on wild fruit and wild honey like the Shankellas, although later on they amassed a large amount of wealth by becoming a scourge to Moslem traders. It is his life in

8

the jungle at that time that made his reputation as a brave fighter. Apparently his band of twelve men had an agreement with another band of seventy highway robbers to share their booty every time they attacked and looted Moslem traders. It so happened that one day the leader of the other band, I think they called him Derar, a man as daring and ruthless as Kassa himself, broke the vow by failing to share his men's booty with Kassa's men. Angered by this, Kassa and his twelve followers attacked the other band, which as I told you was composed of no fewer than seventy men, and inflicted a humiliating defeat on them. Overnight the news spread all over the country, and the name Kassa came to be synonymous with bravery.'

Mulatu paused again, took a gulp of the tella, smacked his lips with satisfaction and went on to say, 'After some time Kassa apparently got tired of his youthful adventures in the jungle and came to settle in this part of the country.'

'Wasn't he afraid of Dejach Goshu?'

'By that time Dejach Goshu was no longer the governor of Quara. Woizero Menen kicked him out and appointed another governor in his place.'

'And how did Kassa settle down? I mean, what did he do?'

'He became an ordinary tiller of land, but that lasted only for a short period. A group of discontented men who had heard about his exploits in the forest came to ask him to give up farming and to lead them into a rebellion against Woizero Menen and her agent here. Kassa readily agreed because he always felt that Quara should be governed by Dejach Kenfu's sons or, if they were incapable of governing the district, by himself. And so the rebels headed by Kassa soon attacked Woizero Menen's agent and chased him out to Gondar. Woizero Menen has naturally been enraged by Kassa's challenge, and we are now waiting to see what action she is going to take against the rebels.'

At this juncture Gebreye, their son, who had all this time been outside the hut cleaning an old spear, came in. He was light in weight and very small in size, but athletic in build just the same.

'You seem to be happy, son,' Mulatu observed, turning his attention from Aberash to him, and catching him smiling.

'Yes, I am,' Gebreye replied.

'About what?'

'The spear, father. It flies off at a jerk of the hand. It is superb!' he said, taking a seat beside his parents.

'I had it made by a special order at the blacksmith's. You should have seen it when it was new!'

'Its blade is large and can cut deep.'

'The edges are a bit blunt, though; they must be sharpened. The tip is a little worn out too, and needs repair.'

'How many people, how many Turks, have you killed with it, father?'

'I don't know, Gebreye, and don't ask me such questions. If I ever killed anyone in my life it was against my will and against my conscience.'

'I don't like to hear about killing, sharp edges, broad blades and the like. They make me feel pain,' Aberash objected to their talk with a distorted face. 'Put that spear away, Gebreye, and bring water for your father to wash his hands with,' she said, and trotted away to the guada to bring lunch.

When the family was around the messob, the round, colourful table made of straw, Aberash addressed her son by saying: 'What is this silly story I hear about you, Gebreye?'

'Silly story? What silly story, mother?'

'That you are preparing to join that man called Kassa.'

'So even you have heard about him, mother! He is great!'

'What are you implying when you say "even you"? That

your mother only knows how to dirty herself in the ash around the fireplace?'

'That's not what I meant, mother,' Gebreye said in an apologetic tone of voice, conscious of his mother's sensitiveness. 'I only meant that such things as fighting are men's business.'

'Yes, yes. Of course. Fighting is only for men. Not for women like me, or for boys like you.'

Gebreye felt trapped by his own argument that fighting was men's business. But then an idea flashed into his mind and he said: 'When Kassa fought against Goshu he was no older than me, mother, and that may prove to you that I am not a mere boy.'

'No, that does not prove anything to me,' she argued. 'If Kassa were a man he would not have run away to hide in some peasant's hut after the battle.'

'Let me intervene and ask you one question, son,' Mulatu said, 'just one single question.'

'What?' Gebreye asked.

'Do you love us, son? I mean do you love your mother and me?'

'How can you have doubts about that, father?'

'Not because I really doubt your love for us. I ask you this question simply to make you realise that you don't know what may happen to us if you join Kassa's force.' He put the roll of stew-soaked enjera into his mouth. 'Our hut will be burnt, and the little property we have will be destroyed by Menen's men if you join Kassa's force and if he is defeated.'

'He won't be defeated, father,' Gebreye replied with absolute conviction.

'What makes you so sure of that?'

'I don't know, but I am sure he won't be defeated. We will fight bravely and destroy the old woman's troops.'

Aberash almost screamed with fright when Gebreye referred

to Woizero Menen, the most powerful woman in the entire country, as 'the old woman'.

'She has a strong army, son. Her followers are as numerous as the grass of Quara and Dembia combined. How can a mere mouse stand against an elephant?'

'You call Kassa a mouse, father?'

'I am only speaking figuratively, son. Kassa is no bigger than a mouse compared to Weizero Menen. I am not questioning his personal bravery. I am, for your information, among the great admirers of Kassa. But he has no army, son, while Woizero Menen has. Believe me, he has no chance against her.'

Gebreye ate in silence for the rest of the time, weighing in his mind his father's remarks. By the time the meal was over he was fully decided to leave home the next day and look for the rebels' camp. He was hypnotised by Kassa, like the rest of the Quara youth.

2

The Rebels' Camp

The rebels' camp was situated on a plateau and surrounded by a wooden fence with four gates. Guards were stationed at each of the four gates. Gebreye was about to dash into the camp when he heard a voice shouting: 'Stop! Stop!'

Gebreye stopped.

'Who are you?' the voice cracked out.

'Gebreye, Gebreye Mulatu,' he faltered. 'I didn't see you, and —'

'Who did you say you were?' the man asked him, coming closer.

'Gebreye Mulatu. I'm Kassa's friend.'

'I'd have carved the entrails out of you if you had made one more move.'

'He thinks he is going to a public house!' the voice of another guard was heard, clucking with mockery.

'Am I in the wrong place?' Gebreye queried apologetically.

'Where do you want to go, kid? And what do you want?'

'I said I wanted to see Kassa. Kassa Hailu of Quara,' Gebreye answered, his embarrassment turning into anger. He disliked being addressed as 'kid'.

'Then wait until you are announced,' the first guard told him, and walked away to Kassa's tent in the camp.

'A stranger wants to see you, sir,' the guard said to Kassa, standing to attention.

'What does he want?'

'I don't know, sir. He says he wants to see you. He is a young, new face.'

'Why don't you take him to Ingida or Gelmo if he is a new face, guard?'

'He says he wants to see you, sir, and he claims to be your friend.'

'My friend?'

'Yes, sir. He calls himself Gebreye.'

'Bring him here, guard. Bring him here quick.'

The guard instantly went back, and told Gebreye to follow him. As they moved inside the camp Gebreye felt he was in a strange place. There were no huts, as in a normal village. The entire camp was made up of tents – big, small and medium-sized tents; red, white, green and black tents; square, round and conical tents. The camp seemed to be populated only with women and children. The men had gone down to the nearby plain for routine exercise, and there were no males in the camp except for Kassa and his personal attendants, such as his shield-bearer. In fact Kassa, too, had been about to leave when Gebreye was announced. The encounter was unexpected and very joyful. Kassa welcomed Gebreye with outstretched hands and embraced him like a younger brother, a brother who had been long lost yet not altogether forgotten. 'I knew you were alive, Gebreye, but God! I couldn't trace you, however hard I tried.'

'It was more difficult for me to trace you than for you to trace me. I have been staying at one place, not too far away from here, ever since I left the Mahbere Sellassie convent, while I understand you have been moving about all the time.'

14

'I have no settled life, Gebreye. I have the presentiment that I shall always be on the move.'

'Well, here I am to follow you.'

'You don't have to tell me that. It's all written in your face. What have you been doing all these years, anyway?'

Before Gebreye gave an answer to this, the guard who had showed him in crept away to his post, greatly surprised by the intimacy of the two men.

'Me? You ask what I have been doing all these years?' Gebreye reflected.

'Yes.'

'I have been milking my father's cows! That's what I have been doing all these years.'

Kassa smiled, and said: 'Seriously, what have you been doing?'

'Nothing worth talking about, Kassa. Only helping the old man run the farm,' Gebreye replied in a regretful tone of voice. 'The only time I enjoyed being at home was the time I sat dreaming about our adventures in the convent.'

Kassa and Gebreye had lived together in the Mahbere Sellassie convent for a couple of years. Gebreye had been taken to the convent because it was his father's lifelong wish to see him become a priest one day. Kassa was sent to the convent because his mother was too poor to bring him up in Gondar, and his uncle Dejach Kenfu thought it best to confide him to the priests.

The priests of Mahbere Sellassie convent admitted both with enthusiasm, believing that the two lads, through the years of schooling and stoic discipline that were the rule of the day, could be shaped up like raw clay into any shape they wanted. While Gebreye was earmarked for the priesthood, Kassa was admitted through the powerful influence of his uncle for general education and upbringing.

It did not take the priests of Mahbere Sellassie convent long, however, to discover what sort of children these two were, these two devils as they called them later on. Neither Kassa nor Gebreye was disposed to pass his time praying like the other children, or poring over books. They were rather inclined to roam about in the nearby woods hunting birds with sling-shots or doing some other mischief.

One day, early in the morning, while all the boys of Mahbere Sellassie convent and their priest-teachers were praying inside the house of God, they suddenly heard a thud on the thatched roof of the church. A young priest in charge of the boys' disci-pline hurried out to check what it was. To his surprise he found Kassa and Gebreye standing in the back yard of the church ex-citedly examining a dying pigeon. The poor innocent creature was gazing at the boys with an accusing eye, blood trickling down its soft grey feathers from its dizzy head where the deadly stone had struck it. The two lads seemed to feel pity for the dying pigeon, but just the same they were happy that they had hit it!

'Who did that?' the angry voice of the young priest was suddenly heard. Kassa and Gebreye almost melted with fright on the spot where they stood examining the bird in its agony. The young priest had approached them from behind so warily that they had failed to notice his footsteps until he was standing beside them. Kassa instinctively ran off as fast as his legs could carry him, but Gebreye felt fixed to the very ground on which he stood. The priest grabbed Gebreye by the arm and gave him a stinging lash on the leg that cut open the tender skin and let the blood flow.

'Who did that?' the priest shouted again, bringing down the whip on Gebreye's leg again.

'It wasn't me,' Gebreye protested. 'Let me go, it wasn't me,' he repeated as the priest brought down the whip cruelly on his bare legs again and again.

'That will teach you a lesson,' the priest told him finally when he let him go. 'Next time you will remember to be with the other boys for prayer instead of killing helpless birds perching on the church roof.' Nothing, however, could correct either Gebreye, who had been whipped, or Kassa Hailu, who had escaped punishment for the time being. The more they were punished the more troublesome the lads became. They were at war with everybody in the convent. They hated the priests for their inhuman punishment and regarded their schoolmates as cowards because of their slavish submission to the discipline of the Church. The two lads, Kassa and Gebreye, raised hell in the holy place. They insulted the priests, knocked the heads of their schoolmates one against the other, tore some precious manuscripts out of malice – for which they had, of course, to pay dearly with the whip – and did all sorts of mischief, until the priests could not bear it any longer. Gebreye was dismissed, while Kassa remained there some time longer, until Dejach Maru sacked the Mahbere Sellassie convent and forced Kassa to run away to his uncle's.

It was a very long time now since Kassa and Gebreye had left the convent. Many things had happened to them both since that time. And yet the memory of it still remained fresh in their minds.

'I just can't forget that incident,' Kassa said. 'I can neither forget it, nor help regretting it.' He was referring to the killing of the pigeon.

'I remember more clearly the lashes I received for it. The marks are still on my skin,' Gebreye said, showing him the dark crescent scars like welding marks on a metal sheet.

'I regret that we killed it, Gebreye. I regret that we killed any pigeon at all.'

Gebreye was somewhat puzzled. He remarked: 'You're not serious, Kassa, are you?'

'Yes, I am serious.'

'You regret having killed a pigeon? Yet I am sure you have killed a number of men since then, and you are certainly going to kill more in future.'

'These are two different matters.'

'Surely they are! Only killing men is much worse, incomparably worse than killing birds.'

'If I have killed men in the past it was always with a justifiable purpose. If I am going to kill men in the future again it will only be with a justifiable purpose. But the killing of the pigeons? We had no purpose in killing them, you and I. We killed them merely out of amusement. And I regret it.'

'Tell me, Kassa, what justifiable purpose did you have in becoming a highway robber, and in robbing and killing peaceful Moslem traders?'

'Oh, that! I had no home, no family. After my uncle died I had to do something in order to keep on living. I couldn't stay at Quara because of Dejach Goshu, who had me chased like a criminal wherever I went. So I had no choice but to fight for existence. Besides, I don't really see my life as a shifta in isolation. It was in a way the beginning of my career. One has to start somewhere, you know. I think I have told you about the prophecy of the monk a long time ago when we were at the convent. I had to start my career somewhere, some time; I had indeed a justifiable purpose in becoming a highway robber.'

'I still have some doubts about it, but I will not argue. I will only ask you now about your immediate plan of action concerning the old woman of Gondar.'

'I just wait to see what Woizero Menen is going to do.'

'By the way, do you know what people say about you and the old woman?'

'You must tell me.'

'Everybody in our district, including my own father, believes that you are not a match for the old woman. They say her followers are as numerous as the grass of Dembia and Quara combined.'

'That's an exaggeration,' Kassa replied, 'but if it's purely a question of numbers we are certainly no match for Woizero Menen's formidable force. But as our folk say, it takes a ball of iron to smash fifty clay jars. That is a true saying, and I have proved it for myself. When I fought Derar's band a couple of years ago my men were no match for his in numbers. The proportion was one man from our side against seven from Derar's. And yet we licked them all. Number is not necessarily the decisive factor in any battle.'

'I wish I had remembered that saying when my father asked me what made me sure that we will punish the old woman of Gondar. I could not explain it to him at that time. I just said, "We shall fight bravely." What I should have said was that it takes a ball of iron to smash fifty clay jars – no, more than that; a hundred or a thousand clay jars.'

'How did your father react to your coming here? Did he like it?'

'He objected to it, of course, and very strongly. But really it wasn't because he dislikes you or anything like that. On the contrary, he revealed to me that he greatly admires you at heart. Only he seems convinced that we will not punish the old woman in the coming campaign, and that the consequences of our defeat will be grave to him because I came to fight by your side.'

'I received secret encouragement from many people, you know. The old folk do not come out with open support because they are not sure how our rebellion is going to end. But secretly they encourage us to go on and fight the Gondar regime. The young ones are of course mad about joining us. Requests to be admitted are streaming in every day, and drilling is going on daily in the plain down below. Incidentally, I am already late. Let's rush down there. You will meet several brave people there, and I will introduce you to my top men, Ingida and Gelmo.'

They left the tent and proceeded towards the gate, followed closely by Kassa's shield-bearer. The guards stood at attention as they passed out. The second guard was trembling.

'You think he will have me whipped?' the second guard asked his fellow guard, when Kassa and Gebreye were a little distance away.

'Will who have you whipped?'

'The master.'

'What for?'

'For having laughed at the newcomer. I took him for a kid, God is my witness. I took him for a kid because he is so small.'

'Come on, don't be an ass. The master does not have anyone whipped for trivial matters. He has much more sense than you think. Besides, he may never know that you laughed at the newcomer in the first place.'

'He is misleadingly small, the newcomer.'

'Forget the whole thing, man. And don't tremble like a little girl.'

The second guard, still trembling, watched Kassa and Gebreye until they disappeared from his sight behind the plateau.

On the drilling-ground Ingida and Gelmo were demonstrating the gugse game – a mock battle – to the new recruits. Both were mounted, each holding a shield and a bamboo stick the size of an ordinary spear. Gelmo galloped ahead, acting as if on the defence, while Ingida chased him close behind, wielding his stick. 'Watch, watch him!' said Kassa to Gebreye. 'Watch him; he is going to get him!' he cried.

Ingida raised his stick, aiming at his mock-enemy, and flung it at a terrific speed. The stick landed on Gelmo's shield and slipped off it to the ground. Both now curbed their foaming horses and swung them around by the rein. Gelmo bent down from his horse's back, picked up Ingida's stick in the twinkle of an eye and started chasing Ingida in turn. He took aim and flung his stick at Ingida. 'No, no. He missed!' Kassa cried, beside himself with excitement. 'His hand caught up in his toga and deflected the direction of his stick!'

'They are as fast and violent as a hurricane,' Gebreye said.

'They surely are. And you must be, too, if you want to come out alive from a battlefield.'

'I am not fast,' Gebreye confessed. 'At least, not as fast as those men over there.'

'You must be, I repeat. And you shall be in due course. Now, when do you want to practise gugse with me?'

'Any time you want.'

'All right. You will rest well today, and we shall play gugse tomorrow,' he said, still watching Ingida and Gelmo.

Ingida and Gelmo were in a sense the true initiators of the rebellion. They were the ones who first went to Kassa and asked him to abandon his farm and lead them against the administration of Woizero Menen, as each had an axe to grind against the present regime.

Ingida was angered by Woizero Menen for removing him from his chieftainship of a tiny district on the eastern shore of Lake Tana. He was charged with misappropriating the tax he had collected from the peasants there, a charge he absolutely denied. The charge seemed very doubtful to all those who knew his integrity. His heart, they testified, was as clean and neat as the white clothes he usually wore. He abstained from all kinds of intoxicating drinks and frowned at those who tried to bribe him. He was a man of great discipline and of high moral standing and not the type to be easily corrupted.

It was true that that year he did not present any revenue in cash or in kind to the treasury of Woizero Menen as he should have done. But his failure was not due to his misappropriation of the revenues. He had in fact collected no revenues whatsoever.

The peasants, having been badly hit by a hailstorm that year, could not even harvest enough crops to carry them over to the next season. And so Ingida, understanding their unhappy plight and sympathising with them, deliberately overlooked the collection of the revenue. As a result he was charged with misappropriation, and recalled to Gondar to be disgraced.

'We are the cause of your downfall,' the peasants wailed at his departure, 'but we shall never forget you.'

For six months following his removal from office he stayed idly at Woizero Menen's court, each day hoping to be forgiven for a sin he had not committed. But Woizero Menen, who enjoyed her entourage of idlers, pretended not to notice his presence at her court. At the end of the six months Ingida could not bear it any longer; he fled to Quara one night to foment trouble there.

Gelmo, on the other hand, was furious at the now ousted governor, who had ordered him to send an ox for the ploughing of Woizero Menen's farm, but who, finding the ox to be of the first class, refused to return it to him. Gelmo would not have minded giving away his good ox to the governor if the governor had compensated him fairly. But the governor, feeling that by right of his position he deserved to own such a good ox, refused either to return the animal to its owner or to pay him compensation for it. Enraged by this injustice, Gelmo resolved to join hands with Ingida and the rest of the rebels and attack the governor.

'This is my friend Gebreye,' Kassa said to Ingida and Gelmo when the latter two came up and leapt off their saddles.

Gebreye noticed something contradictory in Ingida. When he had first seen him from far away, a moment ago, playing gugse, he had taken him for a young, violent person. He now observed that Ingida was not so very young and did not look very violent either. It was in fact a wonder to many that Ingida, who in normal circumstances was so quiet, calm and spiritual in bearing, could handle an arm like a toy and gallop a horse like the devil incarnate.

'Welcome, young man,' Ingida said to Gebreye, examining him from head to foot. 'I didn't catch your name, though.'

'Gebreye. Gebreye Mulatu.'

'Coming from far, eh?'

'About two days' ride from here.'

'Good,' he said, and turning to Kassa asked him whether Gebreye was going to take the oath.

'First thing tomorrow morning, at dawn,' Kassa replied.

The core of the rebels swore on the Holy Bible to fight for the common cause, and to bring down the regime of Woizero Menen and Ras Ali, her son. Whatever personal grudges they had had initially towards Woizero Menen and her governor, Kassa soon convinced them that they were fighting for a higher and a more positive cause. Subsequently they took an oath, thereby establishing a precedent for all future members who would be admitted into the inner circle.

'Welcome to the club,' Gelmo spoke when it was his turn to speak. Gebreye thanked him. He took him for a tough man. Indeed, Gelmo was one big mass of muscle. He was short and broad, almost square. He was firmly built, and gave the impression that he bounced when he moved about.

'Are you continuing the game, or is that all for today?' Gebreye asked Gelmo, eager to watch more of the gugse game.

'That's all for today; I suppose you don't want to see me miss twice the same day?' He laughed good-humouredly.

23

'If you fail to wear your toga properly you are not going to scratch a soul in the coming campaign, Gelmo, let alone wound and kill a soldier,' Kassa teased him, overhearing what he said.

'It does not look as if we are going to have a fight anyway,' Gelmo said. 'Ten weeks have gone by since we sent Menen's governor back to Gondar, and yet nothing has happened.'

'Let's talk about that in the camp where there is more privacy,' Kassa said. It was the rebels' custom to gather in Kassa's tent after their drilling and talk about strategy and the day's activities, or merely sip arake, and joke and laugh.

The rebels could not understand why Woizero Menen had waited for so long before taking action against them. Could it be that she despised them so much that she was not concerned about their rebellion? Or was she waging psychological war against them by keeping them wondering for a seemingly unlimited period of time? Otherwise what was her intention in not raising a finger against them for so long?

'It doesn't surprise me in the least that she has taken no action as yet,' Ingida told the group. He was the only one among them who knew Woizero Menen and her entourage really well. At one time prior to being disgraced he had had a close contact with the Gondar elite. And his idle stay in Gondar for six months had taught him many things about the great woman and her entourage. 'Woizero Menen is not the type of woman who rushes into action,' he went on to explain as they walked towards the camp. 'She takes her time, seeks advice from her generals, and then and only then does she attack if she means to attack.'

'Who, in your opinion, is likely to lead her army against us?' Kassa asked him.

'There are a number of possibilities. The two men who first come to my mind, however, are Wondirad and Bezabeh. But one never knows. She may reserve these two for later campaigns.'

'How do you rate them?'

'Well, Wondirad is a well-known figure. He has put down a number of revolts in Gojam before now. But I don't think he is good at tactics. He just charges like a rhino.'

'And the other one?'

'Bezabeh is more crafty, although I wouldn't say he is a first-class warrior.'

They reached the camp and entered Kassa's small tent. A male servant immediately served them arake, a potent, colourless liquid, and the discussion continued.

'If it's a choice between the two, I mean between Wondirad and Bezabeh, who do you think is more likely to lead Menen's army?' Kassa went on to ask.

'That will really depend on how she rates us. If she believes we are easy to deal with she will most likely send Bezabeh. On the other hand, if she takes us more seriously it will be Wondirad, her favourite general, who will lead her force. By the way, that rhino is an ambitious man, though a blockhead. He is going on all fours in his eagerness to marry Menen's granddaughter, Tewabech, and become a member of the ruling family.'

'We will bury him before he does that. Now let's drink to our cause.'

They all raised their drinking-utensils except Ingida, who did not drink, and gulped the strong spirit down in one draught after shouting: 'To the success of our cause; to the downfall of Woizero Menen!'

3

The Woman of Gondar, I

Woizero Menen was a bulky, elderly woman of nearly fifty. Handsome in features, haughty in spirit, aggressive in talk, she had more of the traits of a man than of a woman; and she was proud of her masculinity. Not on rare occasions did one hear her boast that God had originally intended her to be a man but that for some inexplicable reason he changed his mind at the last moment and deprived her of the male symbol.

What betrayed Woizero Menen's masculinity perhaps more than anything else was her gait. When she walked she trod the ground with the self-assurance of a bull with mighty horns; she walked slowly and heavily, with long strides, as if she were deliberately trying to hurt the very ground on which she stepped.

Woizero Menen loved power and everything connected with it, including such small things as watching people from a raised position. It was for this reason that she so often climbed the upper stairs of Atse Facil castle, her residence since she came to power, and sat – sometimes for hours – on the highest balcony of the massive structure, looking down upon the passers-by. They looked much smaller than their normal size from such a distance, like dwarfs in fact, and this magnified her power over them, which gave her a secret joy.

Her marriage to Atse Yohannes, the nominal emperor, was

again motivated by her lust for power. Otherwise why should she have married him? The pious emperor had neither youth, that quality which enslaves even the most unromantic of women, nor riches, which melt the hardest of feminine hearts. She married him because he had the highest of titles, an empty one to be sure, but the highest nonetheless, a title which legalised her son's as well as her own power.

Woizero Menen and her son Ras Ali were the joint rulers of the country. After the death of her first husband, Ras Alula, and her marriage to Atse Yohannes, she was for some time the sole ruler of the country, as her son was still under age. When he came of age, however, the country's destiny lay in the joint hands of mother and son. Ras Ali could have told his mother to retire from political activities, as he was now in his thirties and himself the father of a young woman, already not only married but divorced. But the idea had not crossed his mind even for a moment.

Ras Ali had a fanatical faith in his mother's intelligence and in her rich experience as a notorious political intriguer. He not only never dreamt of suggesting to her that she should retire from politics, which she would have resented from the bottom of her heart, but on the contrary he let himself be led by her.

Because of this undivided faith and loyalty on the part of her son Woizero Menen enjoyed as much power now as a joint ruler of the country as she had done earlier when she was the sole ruler.

Woizero Menen was furious with the ousted governor of Quara, the day she consented to give him an audience. She was more furious with him than she was with her enemies the rebels. 'You are a coward!' she snarled at him, the moment he opened his mouth to tell her how the rebels had surrounded his home at night, captured him, humiliated him, and finally kicked him out of the district. 'What the hell were you doing when they were surrounding your home? Why didn't you place enough guards? Why didn't you fight them like a man instead of running off like a frightened rabbit?'

'It was a surprise attack, ma'am.' The ousted governor tried to explain to her what had happened, but she wouldn't let him go on. 'Why was it a surprise attack?' she shouted. 'They didn't just gather in an hour and march to assault you, I suppose? They must have been plotting for several days – perhaps for several weeks, or even for several months. What were you and your men doing while the plot was being hatched in the first place?'

'Ma'am, if you would only listen to me for a while I would —'

'It's not that I am afraid of Kassa, or whatever they call him,' she cut him short. 'It is not that. I can send a contingent today, this very moment, and wipe the so-called rebels out. What I find most infuriating is that you, my appointed representative, should run away at the hooligans' command, instead of fighting and meeting your death honourably, then and there.'

'I was not in a posi —'

'Why, why not? That's what I want to know. Why weren't you in a position? Why did you run away like a frightened rabbit, and thereby cause me shame? Why didn't you fight like a man?'

'Ma'am, if you would only listen to me for a moment I would explain to you how it all happened.'

'You are a coward. That is what you are. Now speak up.'

The ousted governor sighed desperately and said: 'It was a surprise attack, ma'am.'

'I heard that already. Don't repeat it again and again like a fool. Go on and tell me the rest of it.'

'The rebels surrounded my residence at night, ma'am, around cock-crow. After forcing their way into my house they threatened to spear me right there and then, in front of my wife, if I didn't surrender at once. My wife screamed in horror and cried for help, but one of the hooligans slapped her in the face so hard that she spat blood right away. No one could come for help, as the guards were already stabbed at the gate and the villagers were fast asleep. What could I do in such circumstances, ma'am, but obey their command? A man who has been attacked by hooligans cannot be accused of cowardice simply because he runs away to save his life. There was no place for gallantry in the whole business, ma'am. Otherwise I assure you I would have proved to you that I do not lack courage.'

'How did the peasants react to the attack anyway – I mean, the next day?'

'I had no time to see or talk to anyone, ma'am. I was driven out of the district by the band of armed hooligans before daybreak. But the fact that there was no resistance against the rebels in the days that followed inclines me to think that the peasants were not too much distressed by the incident.'

'They're always like that when their burden is light! One has to press them down hard in order to maintain their allegiance.' She went on to ask the governor what the peasants' attitude had been like towards the rebels, and especially towards Kassa, before the attack on him took place.

'Everybody talked about them, ma'am, and took Kassa for a hero. Kassa is said to be a man who knows no fear.'

'What? What?' Woizero Menen stirred uneasily like a venomous snake.

'There is no doubt about his personal bravery, ma'am. He is a true son of his father. In fact, his whole family is known for their bravery!'

This was a revelation to Woizero Menen. 'If that is so we must do something about it,' she said. Soon afterwards she called a meeting to discuss the matter and to try to normalise the political situation at Quara. However dominant a character she might be, Woizero Menen proved over and over again that in a time of crisis she was liberal enough to listen to the views of her close followers before taking a final decision on grave matters.

The conference took place in the large audience hall on the first floor of Atse Facil castle. This castle was built over three hundred years ago by the famous emperor whose name it bears. It was and still is a massive structure with four egg-shaped domes at its four corners. Its domes loom up above a cluster of less imposing castles that have been built by a succession of emperors and empresses who reigned after Facil. The whole group is enclosed by a thick stone wall with a dozen huge gates, and is well detached from the rest of the city.

If one stands at the top of Atse Facil castle one can see the whole city, including the market place; the so-called 'bath of Facil', a huge, dry swimming-basin from the middle of which rises yet another ancient castle; the tomb of Zobel, Facil's war charger; and half a dozen old churches. The whole complex is Gondar, the ancient capital city of Ethiopia.

Woizero Menen's generals lived in the city proper, outside the royal enclosure, and when called for the meeting they arrived one after the other.

The first arrival was Wondirad, a giant of a man who, it was said, had received five thrusts of a spear in one of the scores of battles he had fought, but still refused to die. He was tall and massive, like an oak. A favourite of Woizero Menen, he was considered to be one of the major pillars of her power. His loyalty to her was unquestionable and his physical strength still unchallenged. It was believed that if Wondirad flung a spear up into the air with all his might, it would fall to pieces before reaching the ground. During engagements he killed as many men by a squeeze of the hand as by a thrust of the spear.

Next came Bezabeh, Wondirad's rival. Bezabeh was a small,

thin man with a powerful brain. He was not liked by anyone, though he was respected by nearly all. Even Woizero Menen, who strongly doubted his loyalty to her, had some respect for him, especially for the originality of his ideas. He was so original in his way of thinking that he often surprised his listeners by the suggestions he made in such meetings as the present one.

Three other less senior officers entered the audience hall, followed a little later by Ras Ali, who had just arrived with his following of about a hundred men from Debre Tabor. And finally came Atse Yohannes, the emperor, a Bible with a wooden cover in his hand. Woizero Menen had asked the 'shadow' emperor to be present not with the expectation that he would put forward any brilliant ideas but in order to lend dignity to the conference.

Everybody stood up, and everybody – including Woizero Menen and Ras Ali – remained standing until the emperor was seated. Of course the emperor knew that all this show, all this make-believe was a farce; that everybody despised him at heart, and that all the deference showed to him was a pretence. 'They are all buffoons,' his expression seemed to say, though no word escaped his mouth.

Woizero Menen opened the meeting by explaining the purpose of their gathering, and the background of the rebellion. She then asked the conferees to speak freely and to come out with suggestions as to what course of action should be taken against the rebels. A long and a rather noisy discussion followed. Wondirad, unlike Bezabeh, was of the opinion that the one sure way to get rid of Kassa and his men was to crush them by force. 'I don't believe that Kassa is as dangerous as some people think he is,' he said, looking towards Bezabeh and the ousted governor who sat beside him. 'A hundred men with muskets and another thousand with spears and lances could butcher him and his three hundred or so inexperienced followers. I should say in fact that five hundred or so lancers and spearmen headed by fifty musketeers could wipe them out.'

'I strongly disagree,' shouted Bezabeh. 'Kassa's men are neither so inexperienced nor so petty a force that they can be squashed like bed-bugs. There are among them men with rich experience in warfare, and younger ones with enough courage to fight suicidal battles at the command of their leader. Am I not right?' he asked the ousted governor beside him.

'Yes, yes. They are devils. They are devils, unafraid of anything.' The ex-governor supported Bezabeh without, however, raising his voice high.

'You are exaggerating, both of you. You are both carrying the rebels on your shoulders, as it were. You are giving them undue importance. They are nothing but a bunch of hooligans who indeed can be squashed like bed-bugs, one by one. I believe the whole of Kassa's force at this stage is composed of not more than three hundred hooligans who don't even have a single musket in their possession.'

Woizero Menen felt like jumping up and kissing Wondirad. He had said precisely what she wanted to hear. But she said nothing for the moment.

'I admit that we are better armed than Kassa, and that our force is larger and stronger than his beyond any comparison,' Bezabeh persisted. 'But still it is my strong opinion that we should avoid any confrontation at this stage.'

'Are you afraid of him?' Woizero Menen blurted out suddenly.

'I am not afraid of him or of anyone else,' Bezabeh took the challenge gallantly. 'You may order me right now, this very moment, to head a contingent to fight Kassa if you want proof. But you ought to be aware of the consequences, ma'am.'

'Of the consequences?'

'Yes, ma'am. Dejach Wube of Tigre is silently waiting for a ripe time to rebel. Dejach Goshu of Gojam is already in revolt. If a large force is tied up in Quara now the consequences will be grave indeed. We may be forced to fight too many battles in scattered places all at the same time.'

'You mean that Kassa should be left unpunished?'

'He should not only be left unpunished; he should be brought over to our side by any possible means.'

'Cowardice. This is cowardice,' Wondirad retorted. 'If Kassa is left unpunished we shall become the laughing-stock of our enemies.'

'You know, Wondirad,' Bezabeh said heatedly, 'you know that we are not debating on personal matters now, you and I. It's not to oppose you for the sake of opposition that I say you are wrong in proposing a direct confrontation. Kassa is an elusive character. If a force superior to his is sent to Quara now he will not even fight. He will retreat to the Sudan border, the ins and outs of which he knows better than any of us here. He will wait there for some time and come back unexpectedly to lead a surprise attack once again. He is elusive, I say. He is not the clumsy bed-bug that you represent him to be. He is rather an astute flea which you can only catch on the sly, with wet fingers. We must therefore avoid a direct confrontation, and try instead to bring him over to our side in another manner.'

'How, in your opinion, can we bring him over to our side?' Woizero Menen asked him, without conviction.

'With wet fingers, on the sly, ma'am. He must – he must – perhaps I am talking nonsense. But, ma'am, he must —'

'What's wrong with you? Speak up.'

'Well, as I said, ma'am, perhaps I am talking nonsense. But you have provoked me, ma'am, by asking me whether I was afraid of him. I repeat that I am not afraid of Kassa or of anyone else; that you may order me this very moment to go and attack him; but, ma'am, I don't believe that this is the right course of action to take. On the contrary, I believe, ma'am, that he must be bribed in order to bring him over to our side.'

'Make your point more explicit,' she commanded him. 'What sort of bribe are you talking about?'

'I am talking of, eh – of, eh – of a marriage bond, ma'am.'

'A marriage bond? Marry Kassa to whom?' she said, greatly puzzled, and looking sideways to catch her son's eyes.

'To your – perhaps I am suggesting something monstrous, ma'am, but you provoked me to speak my mind. And so I suggest, however foolish it might sound, that a marriage bond between Kassa and your granddaughter will solve this problem of rebellion.'

'What?' Ras Ali snapped out suddenly, 'marry Kassa to my daughter?'

Bezabeh lowered his eyes.

Tewabech, Ras Ali's daughter, had been given away to a famous personage, to a Dejazmach to be more specific, at the early age of twelve, child marriage being the custom of the day. Disgusted with the cruelty of her husband during the consummation of the marriage, she ran away to her family only a few weeks after the wedding-day, and would not on any account return to him. She was now still in her teens and under the tutelage of her father. Her first marriage and the subsequent divorce made her free in principle to marry anyone she liked, but in fact the yoke of custom, and her awe of her family, were still weighing heavily on her. She preferred therefore to remain a divorcee until her father gave her away to another man.

Ras Ali turned as black as soot at Bezabeh's outrageous suggestion that Tewabech should be married to Kassa. Who was he, after all, but a highway robber, a mad adventurer who didn't know his limitations? What rebel in the whole history of the country had won such a reward for brigandage? Ras Ali was so angry with Bezabeh that he proposed to his mother, in a whisper, to adjourn the meeting for an indefinite period of time.

Atse Yohannes had not uttered a word from the beginning to the end of the meeting. He sat by the fireside absolutely silent, occasionally tapping at the wooden cover of his Holy Bible with the nail of his forefinger. He was utterly indifferent to the issue at hand, and didn't even listen attentively to what was being discussed. He only started at Bezabeh's proposal of marrying Tewabech to Kassa, and then gave a faint smile the significance of which was not clear to anyone present.

His political life having been dead for long years, Atse Yohannes did not care in the least who rebelled or where. What did it matter to him whether it was Kassa or someone else who challenged the central government of Gondar? He was used by Woizero Menen and Ras Ali as a tool to legalise their regime, a situation he accepted but never liked. Tomorrow, if these two were overthrown, the victor would again use him as a tool. What was the difference between being the tool of one Ras or of another?

When the meeting was over Atse Yohannes picked up the holy book from his lap, adjusted the skull-cap on his head, and retired to his room in the castle to open his Bible and read from it in his lifelong hope that the humiliation he had undergone in this world would be compensated for in the next.

The generals too left their seats one by one, descended the long flight of stairs that went down to ground level, and dispersed to their respective quarters, wondering in their hearts what Woizero Menen and Ras Ali were going to do.

When the conference hall was empty except for Woizero Menen and Ras Ali, both of whom lingered behind intentionally to continue the unfinished matter, she said to him in the most soothing tone of voice: 'I know how you feel, Ali, for I too felt the same way when Bezabeh's proposal first struck my ears. I felt at that time like jumping at his throat and strangling him to death for his foolhardiness. But I am positively certain that his proposal was not meant to dishonour us. I don't like Bezabeh personally, you know, but his ideas, however foolish they might appear initially, are quite realistic on second thought. Anyhow, if there is anyone to blame for his proposal I admit I am the one to blame, for I challenged him on purpose to speak his mind. Besides, now that we, you and I, are alone I might as well confess to you that Bezabeh's proposal was not an unsound one after all. Don't misunderstand me, Ali; it is not that I doubt our strength to crush that lowlander. It is not that. Only I agree with Bezabeh that we cannot tie up an army in Quara at this stage. And so . . .'

'And so my daughter should become the wife of a bandit, a highway robber!'

'Isn't she as much my daughter as she is yours, Ali? Believe me, I am as much tormented by the scheme as you are yourself, perhaps more so. But we cannot let a brave rogue fall into the hands of our enemies. For the sake of political expediency we must bring Kassa over to our side by any means available. He is brave, they say. Everybody is talking of his bravery. That's one great quality in a soldier, in a warrior, that we cannot overlook. And so I am more and more convinced that it will be an asset to bring that man to our side instead of attacking him.'

'We cannot pay so high a price for that, I mean for bringing him over to our side, if that is what we must do. There must be some other way of making him put down his arms and join us instead.'

'Well, come up with an alternative suggestion that may swing the rogue to our side.'

'One possibility is to offer him the governorship of Quara with the rank of Dejazmach.'

'Be more thoughtful, my son. We cannot do that.'

'Why not, if we have to bribe him at all.'

'First of all, because he does not deserve that rank. Dejaz-mach is a title to be offered to loyal men who have served the state for a long time. To confer such a title on the shifta would provoke a disturbance among our followers. They would be jealous and perhaps defect to Gojam or to Tigre and join the other rebels. Bezabeh for one is fuming inside himself because we made Wondirad a Dejazmach while he remains a Kegnaz-mach. But that's beside the point now.

'The other thing is that if Kassa is made governor of Quara his position will be stronger than it is already, and he will soon turn out to be a formidable enemy. Our aim is not to strengthen his position but to weaken it. And the sure way to trap him is through Tewabech.'

Political marriage was not uncommon in the Ethiopian past, nor is it uncommon today. For years it had been used as a weapon with which to emasculate men with brave hearts, and to bring them around to one's side. And so Ras Ali could not persist in his disagreement for long. 'With her rich experience in political affairs mother can't be wrong,' he thought, and finally he agreed.

4

City Gossip

When the matter was made public it became the subject of gossip in every household of Gondar.

'Have you heard the news?'

'Which news?'

'That the son of Attetegeb is going to be wedded to the granddaughter of Woizero Menen.'

'What?'

'Miracles happen from time to time, you know.'

'You are talking of the kosso-seller's son, I suppose? Or of someone else?'

'The kosso-seller's son, of course.'

'I have surely heard of the kosso-seller's son, but I have never met him in my life. I even thought he had died before the kosso-seller herself.'

'I know him. And he is very much alive, indeed.'

'Is there any young man in Gondar that you don't know, and at whose birth you haven't assisted?'

'Well, what do you expect? I am a midwife, after all. God wouldn't bless me with a child of my own, but he blessed me with the skills of a midwife, and thereby made me a second mother of all the children born in Gondar. And how I rejoice when I hear that the children whose mothers I helped in their labour pains have become great men.'

'Did you ever think that the son of the kosso-seller would be favoured so much?'

'As I say, miracles happen from time to time. I remember the day the child was born. His father Hailu came up to my place out of breath to inform me of his wife's condition. "She has just returned from the market place, her face all covered with sweat," he said to me, all excited. "I thought the sweat was a sign of normal fatigue for a woman in her condition. Of course she should not have gone to the market in the first place. I tried to stop her from going, in fact, but she insisted on it as there was nothing to eat in the house. And at last I unwillingly let her go. On her return she was sweating all over. And she was angry at the price of salt, pepper, tef and everything else she had purchased. Things were getting expensive, it seemed to me, because of the new proclamation which increased the market levies. I helped her unload the basket from her back, and slumping down on the floor she complained to me again about the prices of the articles.

' "I then suspected, seeing her pale face, that the day had finally come for her to deliver the child in her womb, and asked her whether I should call you. She said no. I then went out for a while to the shrine where I used to live formerly, because I had an appointment with one of the scribes there. And upon my return I found Attetegeb moaning. She then of her own will asked me to call you," he said to me.

' "Take it easy," I said to him, and asked him whether he would care for a glass of tella. He wouldn't stay for a minute. "It is urgent," he said in his excitement. "We must go immediately."

'He was indeed right, for by the time we arrived there Attetegeb was groaning with pain. I asked Hailu to plant a pole right away so that the poor woman could hold it tight. It eases the pain to grasp an object tightly when one is in labour, you know. Soon a plump child was born.

39

'Hailu had of course gone away after planting the pole, and when he returned after the child was born, he asked me, still in great excitement, whether the baby was a boy or a girl. When I told him it was a boy he raised his eyes up to the ceiling and muttered: "Thanks be to you, God." It was very strange, you know, the way he muttered these words, raising his eyes to the ceiling. It was as if he would have hanged himself or something like that if the baby had turned out to be a girl. Later on I heard from Attetegeb that he had a reason for his excitement. She told me it had something to do with that monk who passes by Gondar once in a while with his weird tales.'

'That monk is a mystic, they say. He goes without food for a whole month and yet he does not get any thinner by the end of his fast. Anyway, what did he tell Attetegeb or her husband?' the other woman asked.

'I don't remember exactly. But I think he said the child was going to be a big man,' the midwife answered. 'And now everybody says that the son of Attetegeb is going to marry the granddaughter of the queen.'

The Gondares thus gossiped about the proposed marriage and the things related to it for a long time, some with interest, others with envy, and still others with sheer wonder. If there were anyone, however, to whom the news was not pleasant that someone was Kassa Hailu himself. 'Why?' he questioned, 'why me, of all people? Ha! ha! I know why. They want me to betray the cause! Put down your lance, Kassa, marry the beautiful daughter of Ras Ali, become rich and a member of the ruling family, sell yourself body and soul to Woizero Menen and Ras Ali, and commit political suicide! That's it! That's what Woizero Menen wants me to do, to betray the cause and to commit political suicide!'

What was the rebels' cause? Did they have a cause at all? Did they fight for anything? They surely did. The rebels' major objectives were: to pull down the government of Woizero Menen and of Ras Ali; to reunite the dismembered provinces of the country; to re-annex the lost territories on the Sudan border and the Red Sea coast, now both under the hands of the Turks; to rebuild, in short, the Ethiopian Empire that was, and to lead it to fame and glory as in the days of Atse Facil. This was in brief their cause, their ideology.

The core of the rebels, under the magic influence of Kassa, very soon turned out to be patriots, a group of nationalists who became aware that the anarchic situation that existed in mid-nineteenth-century Ethiopia was caused by an ideological vacuum created by the Messafint – the warring princes, Rasses and Dejazmaches. And their cause was intended to fill in that ideological vacuum and to give the country a new sense of direction.

Kassa Hailu summoned his chief men to what he called an 'urgent meeting' in his tent the same day he received Menen's peace terms. He kept his feelings about the matter to himself and announced the news to his co-rebels:

'All sorts of rumours have been going on the last few weeks concerning the action Woizero Menen was going to take against us,' he said to them, 'and now finally I have received the official message from Gondar.'

None of them had expected a peaceful message from Gondar. They were, on the contrary, convinced that Woizero Menen would send an army to try to crush them by force. The mere mention of a message which implied an alternative course of action on the part of Menen was therefore a surprise to all of them, and made them impatient to hear the contents of the message. Kassa explained to them the proposed terms of peace, including of course Menen's offer of Tewabech's hand to him if he agreed to abandon his rebellion.

The first man to react to the news was Ingida, who was

seated beside Kassa. 'It is great news indeed,' he commented. 'It is great news because the Gondar regime has openly recognised our existence as a power to reckon with. But then, there is a point that needs clarification. Why didn't she, as we all expected right from the start, send an army to try to punish us? I am sure it is not because she is afraid of us. She must have some other thing hidden in her mind.' Ingida was deeply suspicious of the scheme.

'I suppose she has been scared by the fact that the peasants of Quara showed no resistance to us. She must have realised that the people silently supported our rebellion.' Gelmo failed to perceive the depths of the scheme.

'I very much doubt whether she was scared of the people's silence, Gelmo. Woizero Menen is very well aware of her might.'

'Whatever her motives might be, she has offered us peace terms, and I think we should accept her offer.'

'No, Gelmo, no,' Kassa's voice came decisively. He was unable to contain his feelings about the proposal. 'Woizero Menen wants us to betray our cause, to cast everything we stand for down the drain.'

'But we may accept her terms of peace without betraying our cause,' Gelmo replied.

'How, Gelmo? Don't you see the poison wrapped up in the sweet terms of peace?'

'That you will be expected to show loyalty to the Gondar regime once you get married to Tewabech? Is that it?'

'Precisely so.'

'If that were the case I would rather be inclined to support Gelmo's view,' Ingida broke in. He was still suspicious that Woizero Menen had something else buried in her mind. It could be that she simply wanted to lull them into inaction so that it might be easier for her to deal them a hard blow all of a sudden.

'I am sure that her sole intent is to tempt us to betray the cause.'

'In that case we have to accept her proposal, Kassa. That is in fact the surest way of enhancing the cause,' Ingida further expressed his views.

'Are we talking the same language, brothers? Is it possible to enhance a cause by betraying it at the same time?'

'It is possible in this case, Kassa,' Ingida went on. 'If you marry Tewabech it is most likely that Woizero Menen will make you a Dejazmach and a governor of some big province. As a Dejazmach you will exercise greater power, and will have thousands of followers instead of only a few hundreds as we are now.'

'Not only that,' Gelmo added, 'when you are the son-in-law of Woizero Menen and Ras Ali not only the people of one district but the entire nation will come to regard you as a possible future leader of the country.'

'But there is one important point you two seem to overlook; that Tewabech will not allow me to stand against her own family, if I go ahead and marry her. What do you say about that?'

'A woman's allegiance to her parents ceases the day she is wedded,' Ingida said.

'I beg your pardon!' Kassa was not convinced. 'A woman's allegiance to her parents never ceases. Not in our society.'

'It will, in this particular case,' Ingida went on. 'Woizero Menen and Ras Ali want to marry Tewabech to you not for her sake, not for her happiness. They want to marry her to you for their own selfish ends, i.e. in order to perpetuate their political power. They are in fact selling her out. And if Tewabech is aware of that, and I see no reason why she should not be aware of it, her allegiance will not be to her family but to her husband.'

'What if her allegiance does remain to her family?' Gelmo

exclaimed in a further attempt to disperse Kassa's fear. 'The worst that can happen will be that you have to divorce her. And divorce or no divorce, your marriage to Tewabech will undoubtedly advance our cause a step further.'

'Now let's turn the coin the other way round, and see what will happen if I reject the offer.'

'There will definitely be a showdown,' Ingida replied. 'But I don't really see why we should fight a battle which we have already won without throwing a lance, without bleeding a soul. We have won the first battle without fighting it.'

'We will lose the good opinion of the public and the people will start to consider you as an arrogant fool who deserved punishment, if we reject the offer,' Gelmo added.

Kassa went into deep reflection. He could not go it alone, ignoring the reasonable views of Ingida and Gelmo. He had to reconsider his earlier silent decision to decline Menen's offer. Finally he said to them:

'All right, I give up. We shall accept Menen's peace terms. But be it known to you all that this is not a reconciliation. We will only be playing the game Woizero Menen's way.'

Throughout the meeting Gebreye looked at the speakers in turn with great fascination, not daring to breathe a word, as he was still a novice without any experience either in warfare or in meetings of this type. Nevertheless he wished deep in his heart that it had been decided in favour of a showdown rather than in the acceptance of the peace terms. He felt that they were there to fight, not to talk about peace or about marriage.

5

The Wedding and its Aftermath

The wedding took place in Gondar city. It was as grand and pompous as might have been expected. The fact that it was Tewabech's second wedding did not in any way reduce its glamour. If it had been her tenth Woizero Menen, out of sheer vanity, would have made it appear as if it were her first. Nearly three-quarters of the Gondares were invited, or rather ordered indirectly to come to the feast. Dozens of bulls, scores of sheep and hundreds of chickens were slaughtered. Honey wine, tella and liquor were brewed generously, to treat thousands of guests. And the costs were, of course, born by the peasants, whose burdens were increased by such memorable occasions. The feast lasted for several days. It gave many favour-seekers a chance to show their loyalty to the regime by running errands like children, or by serving the invited guests like slaves. It gave a chance also to several disgraced people to find an excuse to appear in the queen's palace with a gesture of goodwill, such as a gift of hand-woven carpets, bulls for slaughtering, mules and horses with complete harness, household goods specially made for this occasion, or expensive decorative objects imported from abroad.

Everything was well noted. Everything was well registered, if not on paper then in the clear mind of Woizero Menen and her entourage. Who came to the feast? Who did not come?

Who brought what? And from where? Everything was meticulously examined, recorded and placed in its proper place.

There was practically no one in and around Gondar who failed to pay homage to the grand queen by not showing up at the feasting ground. If anyone was outrageous enough to decline the invitation, the indirect order in other words, it was among those who lived far out of Gondar. But even among those who lived far off there were only very few who were not seen in Gondar during the week of feasting, and one of them happened to be Ingida.

Kassa, the bridegroom, came to the wedding with several men from Quara, including Gelmo and Gebreye, but Ingida remained behind, and the queen could not help feeling his absence deeply. He was the only one among Kassa's followers who was well known to Woizero Menen, and the one most expected. Could it be that he was afraid of some trickery if he came to Gondar? Could it be that he was so hurt that he hated to see her? Could it be that he had too much contempt for the regime? Woizero Menen was very curious indeed to know why he remained behind while the others came, why he did not take this opportunity of reconciling himself with her.

Wishing to know the reason, out of curiosity rather than anything else, Woizero Menen impulsively thought of instructing Wondirad to talk to Kassa about it, in an offhand manner. But then she remembered that Wondirad disliked Kassa as much as Kassa disliked him, and that Wondirad felt sore at heart because Tewabech had been given away to the rebel, since he wanted her for himself. Political expediency demanded it, and there was nothing to do about it. As a result Wondirad was cool towards Kassa from the very day he was introduced to him; he was formal, and even antagonistic at times. It would be no use, therefore, instructing Wondirad to find out from Kassa why Ingida hadn't come for the wedding feast. Woizero Menen

46

could have asked her son-in-law directly herself why Ingida remained behind, as their relationship was patched up now, and there was nothing shameful in doing so. But she was too proud to ask him directly herself. She wanted to avoid a tête-à-tête with him at such an early stage. So instead she picked on another person who could execute the errand in a crafty way. She chose Bezabeh for this purpose.

Bezabeh waited for the right time to broach the subject. He waited till he found Kassa in a relaxed mood, when he was not suspecting anything. He found him in such a mood one afternoon when he and his men were strolling in the city, looking at people and places. He caught up with them when they arrived at the famous Gondar market where Kassa used to do all sorts of mischief in his childhood days. It was there he used to approach a trader stealthily from behind, pick a few fresh lemons or peaches from a basket and fly off like a bird with his loot. The fruit sellers would curse and run after him, but in vain. At other times his loot consisted of roasted grains brought to the market for sale, or green corn-cobs. Whatever the loot, it was a great adventure for Kassa to run away with it uncaught.

'What are you looking for in an empty market-place today?' Bezabeh said in a very friendly tone, after greeting Kassa and his suite. 'Don't tell me you are on a visit.'

'We surely are. It's not pleasant to be in the court all the time, doing nothing.'

'You are right, at times it might even be boring,' Bezabeh agreed, and without letting the friendly atmosphere pass he quickly added: 'By the way, I meant to ask you several times why Ingida didn't come with you. You could have felt more at ease and more at home if he were here. We were all expecting him, you know.'

'Well, I am no stranger in Gondar, Bezabeh. Gondar is my

47

home, my birthplace, and I don't really need anyone to make me feel at home.' Kassa placed himself on the alert, like someone treading a thorny ground bare-footed.

'I didn't mean Gondar, the city as such. What I meant is that you could feel more at ease in the queen's court if Ingida was around. He knows everybody, and despite the trouble he caused the queen by running away to Quara everybody likes him still.'

'Do you believe he made a mistake in running away from Gondar?'

'Not exactly that. But I do believe he made a mistake in failing to carry out his duty and in subsequently losing his post.'

'That only shows that he is a man of principle.'

'No doubt. No doubt about that. But the fact remains that he made a victim of himself by being too lenient to the peasants. Why didn't he come along with you anyway? We were all expecting him.'

'He was not particularly keen about coming, and he has some work to do, besides,' Kassa replied vaguely.

'What sort of work could he possibly be doing while you are away? We would all have liked to see him at the wedding party.'

'He has some work to do,' Kassa repeated as vaguely as before. He was not willing to disclose to Bezabeh that Ingida had remained behind to take care of the camp, and to recruit more youngsters for any possible eventualities.

Bezabeh was preparing to ask more questions in a further attempt to find out about Ingida when to his disappointment they suddenly heard the frantic voice of an old woman trudging behind them. Kassa could not recognise the woman from a distance, and not even when she finally arrived and stood before them, because she was so aged since he saw her last, a long, long time ago, before his departure to Mahbere Sellassie convent. She was bent forward, and her face was a network of wrinkles.

48

'God can be so kind, my son, and yet so cruel at the same time,' she said with tears in her eyes. It was the old midwife.

Kassa could recognise her only by her voice. Although it was trembling, her voice was the same old, motherly voice.

'God can be so kind,' she repeated, her eyes meeting his. 'God can be so kind and yet so cruel at the same time.'

'Why do you say that, mother?' Kassa said like a true son. 'Why do you say that?'

'Why?' she replied. 'Because he has raised you so high, son, and yet took away Attetegeb before seeing this day.'

Kassa and the rest of the group were touched by the kind and sincere words of the old woman. Only Bezabeh was irritated by her intrusion. She had made him fail in his petty mission to find out about Ingida by turning Kassa's attention entirely to herself.

Kassa soothed the old midwife by promising to visit her at home, with the intention of giving her a gift. The old midwife did not charge fees for the services she rendered to the city community, but accepted token gifts. Especially now in her old age, when there was no one to look after her because her husband was dead, and she had no son of her own, she accepted gifts more freely than in earlier days.

'You will be sure to come, Kassa? You will, won't you?'

'I will surely come, mother. You may expect me tomorrow or the day after.'

The old midwife was happy at Kassa's reassuring words. She wiped the tears from her eyes and went on her way, leaving Kassa and his suite behind. They watched her walk away for a while, with pity in their hearts, and then they too started walking, turning their steps towards Woizero Menen's court.

Court life was distasteful to any man of action, and most of all to Kassa Hailu. He hated the incessant and monotonous waiting at the court with a crowd of idlers, where he was expected to appear every day. His only solace and distraction was the occasional stroll in the city, sight-seeing and meeting the common people and talking to them.

His hope in the beginning was that Woizero Menen would give him a new assignment soon after the wedding day and let him leap into some useful work. But instead she kept him idle for months, without even suggesting to him what job was awaiting him. Every day he went to the court with the hope of coming back with something new. But every day he retired home disappointed.

At the end of several months he could not endure the situation any longer. Finding out from Tewabech the hour when Woizero Menen would most likely be alone he went straight to her palace, as he had free access to it, and bluntly asked her why she had kept him idle in Gondar for so many months.

'You must learn patience, young man,' she said to him, as if she had been all this time testing his patience.

'I have waited for seven months, ma'am, doing nothing but warming a stool in your esteemed court.'

'There are people who do wait for seven years!'

'I certainly don't wish to be one of them, ma'am.'

'Are you defying me?'

'I cannot defy you, ma'am, for you have contained me in Gondar.'

'Then learn patience,' she said to him sternly, and in the same breath added: 'I will have you called before long, though.'

Kassa left the palace more restless than before, and feeling somewhat helpless.

Another frustrating month passed by, and yet another. At the end of a third month (the tenth since he departed from Quara) he was summoned to the audience hall of Atse Facil castle. In the presence of Ras Ali and a few other men of rank, Woizero Menen said to him: 'You know, Kassa, that of late the

Turks have been encroaching far into the interior from our western border.'

'Yes, ma'am, and it's high time that someone checked them.'

'I suppose no one would be better than yourself for this important assignment.'

'That's for you to judge and decide, ma'am.'

'Take all the men you have brought along with you from Quara, and teach the Turks a lesson. That's your assignment for the time being.'

Kassa Hailu bowed low in simulated gratitude and left Woizero Menen. He was, however, burning with rage inside himself, for Menen had failed to confer upon him the title not only of Dejazmach, but even of the less attractive Kegnazmach.

If Kassa was disappointed with Woizero Menen, that is because he underestimated her intelligence. Menen was a shrewd, calculating woman whose mind only few of her closest followers could penetrate. Many mistakenly thought that her decision to assign Kassa to lead an expedition against the Turks was based on her belief that only a man of Kassa's calibre could defeat them. In fact, however, Menen was only trying to get rid of this 'dangerous' man whom she deeply feared and disliked. Menen would not forgive Kassa for forcing her to make peace with him at the price she had paid. Her decision to give him Tewabech in marriage was perhaps the best course of action she could take, given the circumstances of the time. But all the same she would not forgive him for pressuring her into proposing to him such terms of peace.

Her primary intention now, in assigning him the task of leading an expedition against the Turks, was simply to get rid of him. She hoped, deep in her heart, that the Turks would either kill him, or short of that maim his body. Thus arose her scheme to send him out to fight the fierce Turks ill-armed and with only the men who had accompanied him to Gondar.

Kassa's friends and followers were as enraged with Menen as Kassa himself. Some went even so far as to suggest to him that he should turn down the assignment.

'I cannot turn it down, and you must know why,' he said to them. 'First of all there is a question of honour involved; if I turn down the assignment Woizero Menen will think that I am afraid to fight the Turks. And then she will have us all thrown into jail where we will rot for the rest of our lives. If we were at Quara it would be a different matter. But we are in Gondar and there is no way of escape for us. And finally,' he went on to say, 'fighting the Turks is part of our original plan. We must re-annex our fatherland.'

Kassa's followers were not too happy about the expedition. Still less were they enthusiastic about it. 'If there is no other choice we must bow to Woizero Menen's decision,' their faces seemed to say. And for lack of any other choice they did bow to her decision.

If anyone was at all pleased about the expedition, it was Gebreye, son of Mulatu. He had not as yet taken part in any battle, and he was eagerly waiting for a chance to come. Now the chance had come, and he was happy about it.

6

Battle of the Border

Tewabech passionately wanted to accompany Kassa to the
Sudan border, but Kassa said no. It was not customary for a
wife to go to the battlefield with her husband. The usual prac-
tice was for the wife to remain at home and for the 'servant-
mistress' to accompany her lover to the war front in order to
wash his feet in the evening and warm his bed at night. Kassa
had two such mistresses back at Quara, and if rumours were
true he had two illegitimate sons, one from each. If he had been
at Quara he would certainly have taken one of them to the
border, but in his present position he could not summon either
of them. On the other hand, he could not allow Tewabech to
accompany him for fear of exposing her to danger. She, on her
part, insisted on going. 'You will need me to dress your wounds
in case of casualties,' she told him before his departure.

'I won't even be scratched, Tewabech, don't worry about
me,' he said to her. 'What I would rather like you to do is to go
down to Quara and wait for me there; don't expect any man-
sion, though, for I have none. For the time being you will have
to be content with living in a tent. Then with the aid of Ingida
you can put up some houses and wait for me there until I
return.'

Tewabech unwillingly agreed to carry out her husband's
wishes and was preparing for departure a few days later, when

Woizero Menen, being informed of her granddaughter's intent, arrived unexpectedly to pay her a visit at her new home. Since their wedding day Kassa and Tewabech had been living in a new compound with a number of houses, outside the royal enclosure. The whole place had been given to Tewabech by Ras Ali as one of her wedding presents.

'How are you doing, my daughter?' Menen asked Tewabech in a pretentious grandmotherly tone, when she was seated in a large stool in the drawing room. She sat on it so solidly that one felt the legs of the stool would sink into the earth floor if she remained in that position for as long as a few minutes.

'Fine. I am fine, mother. And I am preparing to go,' Tewabech answered.

'Go where, my daughter?' Menen asked her, as if she were totally ignorant of what was happening.

'To Quara, of course.'

'But you haven't mentioned that to me before. Were you planning to just run away without even saying goodbye to me?'

'I had no intention of running away without saying goodbye to you, mother. I was only too busy with the preparations to come and tell you about it.'

'Does Ali know about your plans?'

'He does. I sent him a message to Debre Tabor.'

'And he agreed that you go?'

'Of course he did. Why shouldn't he?'

'I don't myself think it advisable that you should go away so soon. Kassa can join you here after his return from the border.'

'My wish was to be at his side at the front. But he wouldn't allow me to follow him,' Tewabech said sadly. 'Instead he asked me to go down to Quara.'

This implied that Tewabech was emotionally involved with Kassa, and Menen was disturbed by it. 'I still think it would be advisable for you, my daughter, to wait until the outcome of the battle is known. It would be useless for you to go down to Quara at this stage.'

Tewabech did not catch the implication of Menen's statement. Still less did she suspect Menen's passionate desire to hear of Kassa's death on the battlefield. She only remembered his sure voice that re-echoed in her ears. 'Don't worry about me, Tewabech, I won't even be scratched.'

'I will be leaving tomorrow,' Tewabech said in a decisive tone of voice which Menen did not like at all.

'You have even fixed the date without asking my advice?'

'Yes, tomorrow I shall be gone.'

'Well,' Menen finally said with a heavy heart, 'I suppose I cannot prevent you from doing what you want to do.'

'Do you really have any objection to my going, mother?'

'It's too late to ask that question, Tewabech. You should have informed me about your plans a little earlier,' Woizero Menen said, rising from her seat to go.

'If you have any objection . . .'

'Well, as I said, it is too late now,' Woizero Menen interrupted her. She dragged herself out of the house, her face dark with anger and disappointment, while Tewabech went back to her preparations for her departure the next day.

A few days later Tewabech arrived at her destination, together with her slaves and personal attendants. Ingida did his best to make her feel comfortable, although it was certainly not easy to do so for a young woman who had been pampered all her life by all the luxuries that befitted a woman of her status. With the help of the young rebels who had stayed behind in Quara and the newly recruited ones he put up a number of houses for Tewabech and her attendants. He had a strong thorn fence built all around her quarters inside the camp and assigned personal guards for her. Finally he too left for the Sudan border to join Kassa in his campaign against the Turks. Ingida was clever enough to suspect that there was something fishy about the expedition. What made him suspect Menen's malice was the fact that Kassa was sent out to fight the fierce Turks with only the couple of hundred men that had followed him to Gondar. Tewabech, on her part, had confessed to him that she was indeed worried about the whole scheme and urged him to raise as many men as he could and join her husband at the front.

In the meantime, Tewabech got well settled in the district. The peasants who lived in the area proved to be very cooperative and ready to obey her slightest command. After all, she was the granddaughter of Woizero Menen, the daughter of Ras Ali, and the wife of a rising star. Who would hesitate to cooperate with a lady who was beautiful and kind on top of all that!

As time went by the peasants living fifty miles or so around came in fact to regard her as their new leader. Some brought litigation to her, ignoring that there were other officials assigned for this purpose or by-passing them outright. Tewabech, who was neither versed in Ethiopian law nor familiar with the existing legal procedures, resorted to reconciliation in such cases, and more often than not she succeeded in her attempt.

Life in Quara was exciting enough for her; it was a new experience. But she was worried about her husband and the possible outcome of the campaign. All sorts of unverifiable news reached her ears from time to time. Sometimes it was that the victory had gone to the Turks, and that Kassa and some of his men had been captured; at other times it was just the opposite. What was most annoying to her was that these rumours could not be verified in any manner. If she could only know the exact situation one way or the other her heart would be at rest. As it was, however, her heart was hanging in the air, so to speak, unsure of anything, until one afternoon one of her slaves, who was splitting wood outside the enclosure, came running in to inform her that a large group of men – some on horseback, others on foot – was heading towards their home. Tewabech was spinning cotton at the time, the usual hobby of high-class ladies. She laid aside her spindle at the slave's news, called out to her maidservant to put away the wicker basket full of white fluff, and rushed out to see who the approaching men could be. She met them at the outer gate. Not one of them was smiling. She saw swollen faces; hands bandaged with dirty rags; open wounds on the legs; some men limping, others moaning with pain. She surveyed the soldiers with her eyes but the man she was looking for was missing. His horse stood aside, sniffing the air and neighing, its saddle empty.

'Is he captured?' she asked Gelmo with a restrained sob. 'Or is he killed?'

'He is with us, madam,' he answered, pointing towards a stretcher carried by four men. 'He will be all right soon.'

The battle of the border, it turned out, had been a disaster. The ill-armed warriors had rushed on the enemy's cannon shots like moths dashing into lanterns. 'They are brave men,' the Turks commented, 'but they are uncouth.' Most of them were killed, others captured, still others seriously wounded. The remaining soldiers returned to Quara carrying their leader on a stretcher.

Tewabech did not waste much time thinking about the lost battle. She sent immediately for Amede, the well-known physician who had once operated on Mulatu's knee, to treat the wounded; and she mobilised the peasants to assist in feeding and quartering the soldiers.

Amede examined and re-examined the wound in Kassa's flank. Finally, covering it up as if in despair, he said: 'Nothing to do.'

'Wh-what do you mean?' Tewabech faltered, her heart sinking.

'It's a ball; I can't extract it,' he replied decisively.

'You will let him die?'

'He won't die, madam. He will recover. But the ball will remain in his flesh for the rest of his life.'

'How can he live with a ball in his flesh?'

'Many warriors do live with balls in their bodies, madam.'

Tewabech could not believe him. She thought he was only trying to console her for the time being. Seeing that she was not convinced the physician said: 'Believe me, madam, he will be all right soon. But you must feed him well so that he may soon recover the lost blood. He lost a lot of blood. That's why he is weak now. But soon he will be all right.'

Tewabech could not hide her emotions any more; she wept for joy.

'Where are the others?' Amede asked, collecting his tools: the horn of a goat with the pointed end bored, a sharp, knife-like instrument, strands of horsetail, and other implements.

'They are everywhere in the village,' Gelmo said, and led him out to the huts where the wounded soldiers were lying. Gebreye was one of them. Among other injuries he had received, the bone of his left hand was fractured.

Amede, after examining all the injuries Gebreye had received, asked Gelmo to fetch him a bamboo pole, to cut out a few internodes from it, and to split the internodes into various pieces. When the pieces were ready he attached them one to the other with strings to form a sort of a miniature raft and, finally adjusting the broken bone in Gebreye's hand, he kept it in position by wrapping the bamboo raft round it and tying it tightly with string.

Gebreye groaned with pain all the time, until the physician said to him: 'Eh! are you a man or a woman? I thought you took after your father!'

'What do you know about my father?' Gebreye replied in anger, his face contorted with pain.

'Why, you don't remember me?'

'I have never seen you before in my life,' Gebreye said, and cried out loud as the physician tightened the string round the raft.

'Open your eyes wide and you will surely recognise me. I am the man who saved your father from near death. And – well, your father is a brave man. He didn't flinch for a moment the day I cut open his swollen knee with the splinter of a broken bottle. He didn't cry even when I put a twig inside his flesh and stirred the pus so that it would come out to the last drop.'

'So it's you!' Gebreye hissed, remembering what people said about Amede – that he was the cruellest human being living in the land.

'You seem to dislike me, Gebreye, judging by the way you are looking at me. But you will like me tomorrow when your wounds heal. I can't be too soft to my patients and cure them at the same time. That's impossible, believe me. I have to be a little heartless in treating them; otherwise I wouldn't be able to cure them.' He fixed a suspender for Gebreye's hand, and returned to Kassa's place to reassure Tewabech that her husband would be all right.

Kassa indeed recovered soon. The moment he was able to talk he sent a message to Gondar to inform Menen of the disastrous outcome of the battle and of his own physical condition as well as that of his remaining men. He thought this was a good opportunity to test her feelings towards him, as he was not too sure of them yet. He instructed the messenger to inform her particularly that the physician had advised him, and the other wounded warriors, to eat plenty of meat to recover their lost blood and energy.

Woizero Menen quite naturally expressed no sympathy for Kassa or for his followers on hearing the message. She was, on the contrary, disappointed that the Turks had failed to kill Kassa.

'What exactly does he want now?' she asked the messenger with an unconcerned and even contemptuous tone, after listening to the message.

'He must be expecting a bull, ma'am,' put in Bezabeh, who happened to be present at the time.

'I am asking the messenger,' she shouted at him.

'I don't know, ma'am,' the messenger replied. 'He just ordered me to report to you what I have just reported.'

'In that case you will take him a joint of meat by which he may totally recover his lost blood.'

Bezabeh sighed desperately on hearing these words. Unable to contain himself, he said: 'That will cause fresh trouble, ma'am. If you are not disposed to send him a bull then send him at least a sheep. It's an insult to send a joint of meat to a warrior of Kassa's standing.'

'What!?' Woizero Menen snarled at Bezabeh. 'Who do you take him for? An emperor, perhaps? A joint of meat is more than enough for a lowlander.'

'He is your son-in-law, ma'am. You are degrading your own honour, the honour of your son, and that of your granddaughter by sending him a joint of meat. Besides,' Bezabeh went on, 'Kassa led an expedition in your name. That he lost the battle is another matter; the fact remains that he led an expedition in your name.'

'From now on you will give your opinions about such matters only when you are asked to do so,' Menen furiously spoke out. 'Until then you will shut up. And you may now leave,' she said, showing him the door.

Bezabeh left her with downcast eyes, feeling totally crushed. He knew he had made an error in speaking so frankly, although he was convinced that the joint of meat was going to provoke fresh trouble.

The messenger, too, left Menen immediately. On his return

to Quara with the joint of meat, which was in the process of decomposition, he reported to Kassa word for word the dialogue that had taken place between Menen and Bezabeh.

'You hear that? You hear what my messenger says?' Kassa addressed his friends and followers who were sitting around him. 'This is a clear provocation.'

'Her tongue emits venom,' Ingida responded bitterly.

'I have long suspected her hatred and contempt towards me,' Kassa hissed out, 'but now I have proved it. I vow to God I shall be revenged upon this woman.'

Meat was not lacking in Quara district. The peasants who had formerly supported the rebels in silence brought them provisions without their asking. Even if the people had been unwilling to feed the wounded soldiers, Kassa and his men would have done what other Ethiopian warriors had done for ages; they would have raided the villages and rounded up as many bulls, goats and chickens as their hearts desired. The question was not, therefore, a shortage of food, or a lack of meat in Quara district.

Kassa's expectation from Gondar had been that of a noble warrior who demanded respect for the task he had been entrusted with. It was a simple act of recognition of his efforts on the border. Woizero Menen knew that very well. She knew also that sending a bull to Kassa would make her none the poorer. And yet she sent him not what he expected of her, but an insult instead, a carcass that was in the process of putrefaction by the time it arrived at its final destination. Kassa, raging with anger, ordered the messenger to cut up the meat, and to throw it to the vultures. Woizero Menen's gift could be pleasing only to scavengers.

7

Warriors March

Kassa's wound had hardly dried up when the rebels started marching towards Gondar, singing war songs and brandishing their weapons. They set out very early in the morning, when the ravens were croaking on the treetops, when the sun was still behind the dark mountains, when the eastern horizon was a sea of colours, one merging into the other, creating a hue that was neither totally red, totally green nor totally blue but a mixture of all colours blended together to form an endless canvas, a work of art created by an invisible, unsurpassed and inimitable artist. There were dark spots and bright spots on the eastern horizon, there were rose lines, and purple lines, and golden lines, there were curved red strokes and crooked blue strokes, and there were lines and spots and curves of all colours. But the sun had hardly hatched out of its dark shell. It was still behind the dark mountains teasing the marching warriors who shouted their chants and brandished their swords in the darkness.

The warriors on horseback were at the head of a long line of foot-soldiers. Composed of about four hundred lancers and twenty musketeers, followed by hundreds of shield-bearers, donkey-drivers, woodcutters and grass-mowers, who were followed in their turn by scores of wives and mistresses leading children by the hand or carrying babies on their backs, the marchers numbered not less than a thousand. So marched the Ethiopian warriors of old. They moved en masse when the weather was fresh; early in the morning, and late in the after-noon, and oftentimes at night when that invisible power was generous enough to give light without the burning heat of the day, when the moon was full and the land was cool and serene. That was the time travellers enjoyed travelling without fatigue.

The warriors marched as did their countrymen in the days gone by. They marched. And they made a stop at a convenient place. They pitched their tents. They spent a night or two there, and then repacking their tents and other belongings they marched on to another camp. And they pitched their tents again, only to repack them after a day or two and go on march-ing together with their shield-bearers, donkey-drivers, wood-cutters and grass-mowers, and their wives and mistresses lead-ing children by the hand and carrying infants on their backs. Ethiopian warriors of old were nomads in the true sense of the word, perhaps more nomadic than cattle-driving nomads who stayed in one place to graze and water their cattle for a longer period of time than the warriors.

Kassa and his followers, encumbered by the presence of women and children, marched on slowly towards Gondar. Resting when tired, getting on their feet again when strong, they moved on slowly like the dark clouds in an Ethiopian winter, until finally they reached a place called Chako.

It was towards evening when they arrived at Chako. The in-visible hand was getting ready to dip the invisible brush into the ocean of colours and to draw its lines and spots and curves on the infinite canvas, and finally to produce that masterpiece, that inimitable work of art in the western horizon. The tops of the traditional 'tukuls' were still visible from a distance. The wearied peasants, carrying their hoes on their shoulders, were heading towards their 'tukuls', towards their homes. The cattle boys were dragging their feet behind the satiated animals. The bulls were sniffing behind the heifers, and the he-goats were having it out after a full day of feeding on intoxicating herbs. Collision. Headlong collision. A backward movement. More backward movement. And more backward movement. A stop. 'On your marks!' 'Get set!' 'Go!' Swift as a violent wind two heads crashed one against the other. No blood. Not a scratch. The he-goats restarted the backward movement. More backward movement. A stop. 'On your marks!' 'Get set!' 'Go!' Swift as a violent wind the two heads crashed one against the other. No blood. Not a scratch. The fight went on until one of the goats gave it up, let out a faint guttural sound as if announcing defeat, and stepped aside.

Kassa, who had watched the distracting scene of the he-goats from horseback, finally stepped down from the wooden saddle and looked around for a suitable forum from which to address his troops. Finding a mound nearby, he mounted it. 'This is going to be our camp for some time to come, soldiers,' he said to his troops. 'By now Woizero Menen must surely have heard of our movement, and she must have already sent out a force to intercept us. We shall wait for the enemy here until we get a sign from our scouts of their arrival. As soon as we hear of the enemy's arrival we shall take up our position in the bush over there.' He pointed with his spearhead. 'Since our enemies are surely carrying a large number of muskets and possibly cannons, with which they can attack us from a distance, we shall wait in ambush until they are close enough for a hand-to-hand fight. The last battle has taught us a lesson, soldiers. We shall not rush on the enemy heedlessly and thereby make ourselves an unnecessary target.' He paused, and raising his voice higher he continued: 'A trumpet will be blown as a sign to start the attack on our side. Until the trumpet is blown no one shall move from his ambush. But should anyone skulk behind at the sound of the trumpet, woe to him! I shall have no mercy on cowards. We shall fight the enemy to the last man and cut his force to pieces. Remember, soldiers, that we are fighting Woizero Menen who, without shame, sent us a joint of meat by which to recover from our bleeding wounds after our return from the border, where she had sent us to defend the fatherland. This is a battle of vengeance, soldiers, as much as it is a battle for a cause, the great cause of reuniting the empire that fell prey to selfish Rasses and chiefs. We have a mission to fulfill, soldiers, and we shall spare no effort in accomplishing that mission.'

'We shall fight to the last man; we shall fight till the last drop of our blood is drained out of our veins,' the troops echoed.

A child cried out, frightened by the echoing voice of the troops. Tewabech trembled where she stood. She trembled, not because of the resounding voice of the troops that had frightened the child. She trembled at the mention of her grandmother's name in her husband's speech. She trembled, too, at the word 'vengeance'. For her this was the beginning of long painful days, days in which she had to choose between two heartrending evils. But can one choose between burning a finger or freezing a toe? Isn't the one as painful as the other? Could she be faithful to her husband and to the cause he stood for without being unfaithful to her family? Could she be devoted to her family without denying her husband? The choice was a difficult one.

Tewabech had refused, unlike the previous time, to stay at Quara, despite Kassa's insistence that she should remain behind. All the words of persuasion, all the stories of the dangers of war fell on deaf ears. She refused to stay behind and be tormented by unverifiable rumours. 'From now on I shall follow you wherever you go,' she told him defiantly the day the march started. 'I shall follow you wherever you go, even if it is to the fires of hell.' And now she was trembling, trembling at the word 'vengeance' that was directed against her family.

The troops dispersed soon after Kassa's speech to unload their provisions, pitch their tents and construct bowers for the horses and pack animals. The falling darkness could not prevent them from turning the place into a veritable village in a couple of hours.

8

Braggart of a General

No sooner had Woizero Menen heard of the second rebellion than she summoned her war lords and hastily explained to them the situation. 'Our previous course of action has proved to be a total failure,' she said to them, her accusing eyes falling on Bezabeh. 'Kassa has rebelled again, and this time we are not going to talk about bribes, about winning him over to our side, or any other nonsense. That the lowlander is only a mediocre warrior has been proved by the battle of the border. That he is a man not to be trusted has been proved by his second rebellion. There is now but one course of action to take against him, and that is to crush him by force. I will give this honourable assignment to you, Wondirad,' she said, looking towards her favourite general. 'Take as many muskets and cannons as you require. Only don't let Kassa escape into the wilderness. Dead or alive, I want to see him here in Gondar.'

Menen could not have picked any better man than Wondirad for this 'honourable assignment', as she called it. Since the day Kassa was wedded to Tewabech, Wondirad had come to regard Kassa as his personal enemy; a worse one than Bezabeh himself, because in the first place Kassa had shattered his hope of ever marrying Tewabech, and in the second he was afraid Menen would bestow more favours upon Kassa than upon him, now that the 'lowlander' was her son-in-law. Ever since the wedding day, Wondirad has been thinking of how to incite Kassa to a duel and put an end to him. A number of times the idea of spitting in his face by way of provocation had crossed his mind. But he preferred to wait till he found a more gentlemanly way of challenging him. Now he was happy that the time for confrontation was at hand.

'When a nobody like Kassa is rewarded so much, and so early in life, he usually forgets who he is, ma'am,' Wondirad replied to Menen with an overwhelming passion. 'I suppose everybody here knows the background of this mad adventurer, I mean the incontestable fact that his mother, in her wretchedness, sold the pugnacious kosso in the Saturday market of Gondar.' Some people laughed at this remark. But the laughter was soon hushed down by Menen, who said: 'Oh, yes; how degrading it was for us to give him Tewabech in marriage! And how ungrateful on his part to raise his arms against us! But what has been done cannot be undone.'

'You may count on me, ma'am,' Wondirad went on to say. 'I shall not fail to bring the son of the kosso-seller to your feet, dead or alive.'

Bezabeh felt as much crushed as Wondirad felt elated and triumphant. These two men had for a long time been foes, secretly struggling to gain greater favour from Menen. True, Bezabeh's original suggestion that Tewabech should be married to Kassa in order to bring the latter over to Menen's side had come from his heart. He felt it was a sound suggestion, and Woizero Menen accepted it. But Bezabeh had an additional motive in suggesting it. He was sure that the marriage bond would undermine Wondirad's position. Kassa, he calculated, as the son-in-law of Menen and Ras Ali, would occupy the first position among the generals, and automatically bring down Wondirad to the second rung. His own position would also be lowered, to be sure, but he did not mind stepping down to the third rung as long as Wondirad came down to the second.

Bezabeh now admitted in his heart that he had lost the un-declared war against Wondirad, and that he was doomed. Nevertheless he knew that there was another way of fighting his foe, and resolved to meet him in the hot battlefield.

That same evening Bezabeh started to contact those soldiers who, he knew, were dissatisfied with the administration of both Menen and Wondirad, to incite them to join Kassa and fight against the government. The same night, together with a moderate number of defectors, he set off for Chako to join the rebels.

On their arrival they were spotted by one of Kassa's scouts who, believing that these were the expected enemies, was about to mount his horse and gallop away to alert the rebels when he heard a shout from Bezabeh. 'We are not enemies,' Bezabeh cried. 'We are friends, not enemies.'

'Throw your lance away if you are the friend you claim to be,' the scout shouted back.

Bezabeh threw away his lance and approached him totally unarmed.

'Who are you?' the scout asked him.

'My name is Bezabeh. 1 am from Gondar.'

'And you say you are not an enemy but a friend?'

'Right.'

'How can I believe you?'

'You can just introduce me to Kassa. He knows me very well.'

'Follow me,' the scout said and galloped away to the camp.

'What brings you here, my friend?' Kassa said to Bezabeh, not without surprise, seeing him alone at Chako. 'I thought you might possibly lead Menen's expedition.'

'I have come to fight by your side, Kassa, and I am not alone.'

Kassa looked at him from head to toe with suspicion. 'How do I know you are not tricking me?'

'I have been told that you believe strongly in Christ, Kassa, don't you?'

'Yes, of course.'

'I, too, believe strongly in Christ. And I am ready to swear on the Holy Bible that we have all come to fight by your side.'

'Why do you want to fight by my side? I would like to know.'

'Because I detest Menen, and I hate Wondirad who is going to head the expedition against you.'

'Wondirad? Oh yes! Tell me about his preparations.'

'He will most likely come with a force of over a thousand soldiers, all armed to the teeth. He promised Menen, and he did it in my presence, to capture you and drag you to Gondar. To use his own words, he said: "You may count on me, ma'am, I shall not fail to bring the son of the kosso-seller to your feet, dead or alive."'

'Did he really say that?' Kassa asked him, stung by the abusive phrase, 'the son of the kosso-seller'.

'He did, and very boastfully too. And he made many people laugh.'

'At my cost?'

'Yes, at your cost.'

'All right, I shall not forget it,' Kassa said curtly. He added: 'I thank you for the information, Bezabeh. But I must tell you one thing, that if you came to fight with us simply because you hate Menen and Wondirad I don't want you.'

'What else would you require of me?' Bezabeh asked him with astonishment.

'We are fighting not simply because we hate some individuals. We are fighting for a positive cause. We are fighting in order to rebuild the Ethiopian Empire that was. If you fully accept our cause you are welcome. If not, you have no place with us.'

'I accept everything you say.'

'Then bring along your men and we shall have you all sworn in on the Holy Bible.'

In a brief ceremony Bezabeh and the group of soldiers who came along with him to Chako pledged themselves to fight for the common cause.

In the battle that followed, the battle known as the battle of Chako, Kassa's tactical instructions were followed strictly. Before Wondirad and his men knew what was happening around them, a trumpet was blown, and at the sound of it Kassa's men rose from their ambush. They fell on the un-suspecting enemy by surprise, like a sudden flood that sweeps away anything lying in its course. The rebel force attacked so fast and so effectively that for some time the enemy had no hope of making a proper use of the cannon and of the muskets they carried. As the battle progressed, however, Wondirad's men, getting accustomed to the situation, put up a good defence. Though scores of them had already fallen, their advantage in numbers enabled them even to take the offensive for a brief moment. In the heat of the fight Kassa located Wondirad, all decked in his military outfit, striking right and left with his mighty arms, and at each accurate stroke chopping off a head or a limb like so many leaves cut down from a tree. Kassa, maddened by the dexterity of Wondirad, and possessed by hatred, dashed straight towards him and sank his lance into the flank of his heavy steed. This instantly fell to the ground, fling-ing Wondirad on to the earth behind its tail. Wondirad, slightly hurt, lay flat on his back, his spear and shield jerked out of his hands. Kassa maliciously galloped round and round the fallen horse and master, taunting Wondirad and threatening to sink his other lance into his big stomach. Wondirad lay motionless, his eyes following Kassa's lance, his head swirling and swimming, his heart feeling the earth as it went round and round. Wondirad's men became panic-stricken on seeing Wondirad flat on the ground, unable to rise up and fight. Chaos ensued. Some threw down their weapons and let themselves be captured, while others started to flee in every possible direction. Kassa's men pursued the fleeing soldiers, killing scores of them and taking away their muskets and lances.

The battle soon came to an end, and Wondirad was driven away to the camp together with other captives.

'Why did you spare his life?' Bezabeh asked Kassa as they were riding back to the camp.

'I haven't spared him,' Kassa answered.

'He has been taken to the camp safe and sound.'

'I know, Bezabeh. But I haven't spared him,' Kassa replied, and they continued their ride towards the camp.

In the evening an open-field feast was prepared to celebrate the occasion. Kassa's soldiers started munching reeking raw beef, and emptying jugs of honey wine and tella. In the centre of the feasting crowd sat Kassa, with Gelmo, Ingida, Gebreye and Bezabeh. The bards played tunes on their stringed kerars. Some soldiers, unable to contain themselves, leapt up from the ground and, slashing the air with their curved swords, cried their war chants. In the heat of it all Kassa made a sign to Gebreye to come closer, and whispered something in his ear. Gebreye made his way out of the crowd and headed towards the quarter of the captives. Kassa summoned another soldier and instructed him to fetch a special drink from his own tent. Soon the soldier returned with a clay jar, while Gebreye and two guards arrived driving Wondirad before them like a bull being

72

driven to a slaughterhouse. Too crushed and too humiliated to look Kassa or Bezabeh in the face, Wondirad stood before the crowd, with his eyes cast down.

The crowd ceased feasting for a while, and watched with amusement what was going to happen. When absolute silence reigned Kassa spoke, his eyes fixed on Wondirad. 'I thought it unfair that you should be staying in your confinement while we are feasting and merry-making,' he said to him, tongue in cheek. 'You will feast with us on a special drink which my mother has sent you from her grave.'

The crowd burst out laughing at this juncture, understanding Kassa's cutting words, without however knowing the nature of the special drink. When the laughter subsided Kassa, looking towards the soldier who had fetched the stinking liquid, said 'Fill that wancha full to the brim, soldier, and hand it to Dejach Wondirad.'

The special drink was, of course, kosso, the laxative that people drink in order to get rid of tapeworm. Kassa had had it prepared in advance, in anticipation of victory, in order to have his revenge upon Wondirad, who had insolently abused the woman who had given Kassa life, and whom he adored.

'Gulp it down!' Kassa shouted at Wondirad, who grimaced at the foretaste of the kosso. He then drank it, holding his breath. 'Pour him another one,' Kassa ordered the soldier, who instantly poured the liquid into the empty wancha and handed it over to Wondirad. When Wondirad was halfway through the second refill he hiccupped. 'Swallow it, and quickly,' Kassa threatened him. The crowd watched tensely as Wondirad struggled to force the drink down his throat. It refused to go down. It gushed out instead, sprinkling the nearby watchers.

'All right, all right,' Kassa said in disgust. 'Take him away, guards, but make sure that he finishes that jar before the end of our feast.'

The crowd relaxed, and fell back on its meat and drink. The bards resumed their songs while Wondirad, now among his own captured men, went on gulping and vomiting the kosso until the jar was empty.

9

News of Defeat

The possibility of Wondirad's defeat had not crossed Menen's mind even for a second. Ever since the departure of her general her mind had rather been occupied with one thing only – how to punish Kassa when her war lord finally brought him to Gondar alive. Have him hanged from a wanza tree in the market-place? Have him speared to death standing against the outer wall that enclosed the royal quarter? Or spare his life and let him rot for the rest of his life in the state prison at Sar Amba?

Woizero Menen did not foresee the possibility of Kassa's victory. How could such a thing happen? She had sent an army at least twice as large as that headed by Kassa Hailu, armed with the most up-to-date weapons available in the country at the time. On top of that, Wondirad, that giant of a man, that renowned warrior, had promised her in public that he would drag the son of the kosso-seller to Gondar, dead or alive. How then could the idea of Wondirad's defeat enter her mind even for a moment?

Woizero Menen was sitting on the top balcony of Atse Facil castle, one afternoon, enjoying as usual the sight of the small, dwarf-like creatures moving about in the rubbish-heaped, stone-blocked path that ran from one side of the big stone wall to the city proper, when one of her guards came up hurriedly to inform her that a certain Grazmach Moltot was seeking audience. 'Send him up,' she said impulsively. Apparently she was thinking of someone else. But then suddenly it dawned upon her that Grazmach Moltot had been on the expedition to Chako. 'What news could he have brought?' she reflected. 'Perhaps the lowlander has vanished into the wilderness; or perhaps Wondirad wants reinforcements or provisions.' As her thought thus wandered about desultorily, hitting now on one possibility, and then on another, she suddenly felt possessed by fear, a certain fear the source of which she couldn't grasp. She felt an urgent need to hear the news.

'We have lost the battle, ma'am,' Grazmach Moltot boomed like thunder.

'What?' she said blankly, as if her head all of sudden had banged against a stone wall.

'We have lost the battle, ma'am,' Moltot repeated. 'About one-third of our men have been either killed or captured, including Dejazmach Wondirad; another third defected to the enemy during the battle, and the remaining third is back in Gondar.'

'Enough. Enough. Go away, that's enough,' she said, struggling to her feet.

Woizero Menen would not admit the fact that the battle had been won by Kassa. 'It's the renegade who won the battle,' she consoled herself, as though that were any consolation at all, as she descended the upper stairs of the castle. 'It is Bezabeh, not Kassa, who won the battle! He knew our strategy and he betrayed us. But neither Bezabeh, the masked fox, nor Kassa, the despicable lowlander, will escape my punishment!'

Woizero Menen resolved then and there that she would lead the next expedition herself. With Bezabeh defected to the enemy and Wondirad captured, she could not entrust the heavy task of leading another expedition against the rebels to her second-rate officers. The only other person apart from herself

76

who could take up the assignment with confidence was Ras Ali. But Woizero Menen preferred to reserve him for the last show-down. 'If the impossible happens and I fail,' she told him the next day when they met, 'it will be your turn to take up your arms and wipe the rebels off the face of the country.'

Ras Ali strongly protested against his mother's decision that she should lead the next expedition in person. He would in fact have preferred to tempt Kassa with a title and a senior appointment, instead of fighting their own son-in-law. But his furious mother refused to listen to any terms of peaceful settlement of the worsening conflict. Preparations for the next expedition soon began to be made. Provisions were collected from the groaning peasants, sturdy pack animals were selected, weapons polished, tents packed and tasks assigned to slaves.

Needless to say, similar preparations were under way on Kassa's side, in view of the next inevitable confrontation, when some very unfortunate news reached the camp. A messenger from Quara came to inform Gebreye that his father was seriously ill and that his mother urged him to return home as soon as possible. Knowing his mother well, Gebreye did not take the matter too seriously at first. It could be that she merely wanted to see him after nearly three years of separation, and that she had fabricated an excuse to have him sent home; perhaps Mulatu had suffered a slight stomachache and she exaggerated his condition. On the other hand, Gebreye could not be sure that his father's condition was not as serious as was reported. One way or the other he decided, on second thoughts, to inform Kassa about it and ask permission to go and see his father before the start of the next campaign. 'It's a pity you hear such news at such a time,' Kassa said to him. 'You know that we are going to start our march towards Gondar in about two weeks' time. And I cannot afford to do without you, or anyone else for that matter, as it is certain that Woizero Menen will mobilise an army much more numerous than the previous one.'

'I am not intending to stay with my father for long, Dejazmach. I only want to make him happy by being at his side for a couple of days if he is still alive.'

Kassa's followers as well as his admirers had started addressing him as Dejazmach from the day the battle of Chako was fought and won.

'Are you sure you are not going to stay longer than that?'

'I am quite sure of it, Dejazmach. I am fully aware of the importance of the coming battle, and whether my father is dead or alive I will be back in a few days' time.'

'Well,' Kassa said in a tone of agreement, 'what will you need for your trip, in that case?'

'Nothing, Dejazmach. Nothing at all.'

'But you may need some money to buy your father medicine.' Kassa ordered his personal treasurer to fetch him a bag from a specific box he described as yellow in colour. Upon the return of the treasurer Kassa handed Gebreye a white bag half-filled with silver coins, saying at the same time: 'My best regards to your father. I hope you will find him well so that you may return all the sooner. By the way, don't fail to explain to him the cause we are fighting for. Many people still think that we are mere adventurers seeking fortunes for our selfish ends.'

'I will remember to do so, Dejazmach,' Gebreye replied, and saying goodbye to his friends he left for home.

10

Dialogue with a Priest

Mulatu was suffering from malaria, a disease very common in
hot areas like Quara. The fever came and went intermittently.
When it came Mulatu was bathed in hot sweat, and his entire
body quivered like a tuning fork. The fever usually lasted for
half a day, and then Mulatu's body cooled down. During this
period he could eat, drink and talk like other, healthy people.
Now upon Gebreye's arrival Mulatu was in the happy interval.
He was lying comfortably on the medeb, the raised earth bed,
chatting with Aberash. Gebreye bowed down and kissed his
parents repeatedly on the cheek in turn.

'We had not expected you so soon, Gebreye,' Aberash said,
beaming with delight, and immediately started fussing about
her son's appearance. 'Look, look at him! How he has changed!
His beard was hardly visible when he left us; but look now how
long and how bushy it has grown. And his hair! I swear on the
Holy Virgin he looks like a real shifta, a real highway robber!
Why, why, Gebreye? Why did you let it grow so wild? Upon
Christ, our Lord, he is no longer a boy, he is a man!' she cried,
and fluttered towards him to kiss him on the cheeks afresh. And
she made quite a noise with her lips, a noise like the popping
of a cork. 'We have missed you so badly, Gebreye. And
don't think that your father is perfectly all right because you
see him now comfortably lying on the medeb. I didn't lie

to you about his health – just wait and see him in his bad hours.'

'Don't be apologetic, mother. I hadn't said you lied to me,' Gebreye said, and then turning his attention to his father asked him when it all began.

'Oh, about three months ago, I believe. Am I not right, Aberash?'

'Yes, yes, of course. About three months ago, the day after the annual feast of St Michael.'

'The fever is unpredictable,' Mulatu explained to Gebreye. 'It just comes and goes like a flood, and it gets worse when the moon is full.'

'Are you taking any medicine?'

'I used to, minced garlic mixed with honey. That is what the medicine man advised me to eat every morning before tasting anything else. Garlic is hot, you know, and burns the stomach. But we ran out of cash lately, so I stopped it.'

'Dejach Kassa sent you his greetings, and this too,' Gebreye said, handing him the white bag. Aberash's eyes popped out with excitement at the sight of the bag, and she remarked: 'We thought there was only cruelty in him; didn't they say that he forced the general to drink kosso to his death?'

'No one is kind to his enemies, mother, and no one is cruel to his friends.'

'How well you talk, son!'

'Is that a true story, Gebreye?' Mulatu wanted to ascertain the rumour of the district.

'What?'

'The way Dejach Wondirad was put to death.'

'Yes, yes. It is true. Wondirad died of dysentery, after emptying a whole jar of kosso.'

'By the Holy Virgin, mother of Christ! That was cruelty at its worst,' Aberash exclaimed afresh.

'Stop playing the buffoon, Aberash, and fetch some food for Gebreye. You forget that he has just returned from a long journey,' Mulatu admonished her.

'Today is Sunday, father of Gebreye. Aba Tekle will be here any moment. We shall all eat together, it's a happy day,' she said and trotted away into the guada to prepare lunch.

Gebreye did not like hearing the name of the priest mentioned. Since his painful days in Mahbere Sellassie convent he had been prejudiced against all priests, including Mulatu's father confessor who unfailingly sat at Mulatu's messob every Sunday at lunch hour.

Aba Tekle, the head priest of the parish across the river, and the administrator of vast ecclesiastical lands on which laboured every year some two hundred of the faithful, was a man of middle age, well versed in Ge'ez (the classical church language), and head of about twenty priests and deacons. He was revered in the district, and the faithful considered it an honour to have him in their homes. They revered him so much that they literally believed that winged devils flew out of the house the moment Aba Tekle stepped in.

Aba Tekle arrived at twelve sharp, wearing an immaculate white turban that would no doubt dazzle any winged devils, if such existed. He wore an equally white long dress, and a pair of baggy trousers. Over the dress his shoulder, chest and back were enveloped in a cotton toga which, in turn, was covered with a black cloak with a red lining, open in front. He held a metal Coptic cross chased with fine designs in one hand and a fly-switch in the other.

The fat, experienced devils with long noses and red eyes must have smelt his approach from far and flown out in a rush. But there might have been small ones too who were not so accustomed to the smell of holy beings. So to make sure that Mulatu's house was cleared of all possible imps Aba Tekle stood at the entrance and slashed the air with his cross, up and down and sideways, muttering prayers in Ge'ez at the same time. He then moved to the medeb to bless Mulatu by letting him touch the cross with his forehead and with his lips several times. Aberash, too, jumped out of the guada to kiss the cross. As the guada was the most convenient place for the winged spirits to hide in, Aberash led Aba Tekle into it so that he could bless it also.

All the while Gebreye sat absolutely indifferent to what was going on. Aba Tekle was in fact expecting him to jump up from his seat to kiss the cross. But Gebreye did nothing of the sort. To save face, therefore, the priest went to him and touched his forehead and lips with his silver cross.

Finally, when he was seated, he addressed Gebreye in the most paternal tone of voice possible. 'You must be very tired, my son, to sit down and wait for me to bless you with the cross of our Lord. I am glad you are back home, though. Your parents were so worried about you. They talked of nothing else but of you whenever I paid them a visit.'

Gebreye ignored the priest as if it were below his dignity to talk to him. Feeling embarrassed by the situation, Aba Tekle turned to Mulatu and asked him about his health, and whether he was getting better.

'Thanks be to our Lord, my health is improving fast,' Mulatu said eagerly. He too was embarrassed by Gebreye's unusual attitude.

'Being sick is a blessing from God,' the priest went on to say somewhat naively. 'We are made conscious of the brevity of this life only when we get sick; because of the closeness, or the apparent closeness of death we are reconciled to God through prayer and penance. Is that not true?' he said with a smile that appeared rather stupid to Gebreye.

'It's true. It's absolutely true,' Mulatu promptly confirmed.

Gebreye felt like saying 'Absolute nonsense'; but his lips involuntarily uttered, 'It is not true.'

'There! there! he is going to oppose his own father,' the priest said, happy nevertheless that Gebreye had at least said something. 'Why do you say that, anyway?'

'Sickness cannot be a blessing from God. You attribute every thing good and bad to God. If a man is sick it is a blessing from God; if a man is poor it is a blessing from God; if he is a beggar, again it is a blessing from God. Everything, whether good or bad, is a blessing from God according to you. But this is blaspheming God, for nothing bad can come from God.'

'I didn't mean sickness of itself is a blessing from God, my son. I meant the state of being sick is, for it brings one closer to God.'

'I see no difference between saying sickness is a blessing from God, and the state of being sick is a blessing from God. Besides, people don't have to be sick in order to be conscious of death. They are conscious of it without being sick.'

'But not as much as when they are sick.'

'How about warriors who, so to speak, throw themselves into death? Aren't they as conscious of death as sick people are?'

Aba Tekle could not answer this question readily. So Gebreye went on to say: 'Warriors are more conscious of death than are sick people, or priests. But because they are fighting for a cause they despise death.'

Mulatu, who saw the embarrassed face of his father confessor, was afraid that if the dialogue continued in this way it would end up in still greater embarrassment for Aba Tekle. So he called out loud for Aberash to ask her bring the food. He also said something irrelevant, just to change the subject, but neither Gebreye nor Aba Tekle noticed the remark.

'I could understand what you have just said if all soldiers

were fighting say foreign invaders, like the Turks. But for what cause you and your rebel colleagues are defying the legal government is an enigma to me,' Aba Tekle said in a sort of self-defence, when the food was finally served.

'What legal government are you talking about? There is no legal government in this country. We have lived in anarchy for nearly seventy years.'

'Why, you don't accept Atse Yohannes as the legitimate ruler of the Empire?'

'The Ethiopian Empire is no more, Aba Tekle. And Atse Yohannes is not the ruler of this country. It's the Yeju Gallas, Woizero Menen and Ras Ali, who rule the country, and you know it very well.'

'No matter. Ras Ali is the emperor's guardian, and the emperor has sanctioned the government of Ras Ali and of the queen. Therefore, the present government is a legal one indeed.'

'There hasn't been a legal government in this country since 1769,' Gebreye reminded the priest of the country's history. 'Since that year, since the day Ras Michael Sehoul of Tigre usurped the power of Joas and had him assassinated, there has not been a legal government in Gondar. Ras Ali and Woizero Menen are only deceiving themselves and the people when they call their rule a legal one.'

Aba Tekle was by no means ignorant of the country's history. But like the rest of his fellow ecclesiastics of the time he tried to cover up the truth, allying himself with the ruling clique in order to safeguard the Church's interest as well as his own. He supported Woizero Menen and Ras Ali now because they were stronger than the rebels. If things were to be reversed tomorrow, however, he would no doubt applaud the victors once again to safeguard the Church's interest and his own.

'So you think, Gebreye, that you are fighting for a great

84

cause while in actual fact you are only defying the legal government?'

'I repeat that there is no legal government, Aba Tekle, and that we are indeed fighting for a noble cause,' Gebreye answered rather heatedly, almost biting out each word of his statement for emphasis. 'Incidentally,' he added, turning to his father, 'Dejach Kassa asked me to inform you that we are not fighting for selfish motives, but that we are sacrificing our lives, in contempt of death, in order to restore the ancient glory of our country.'

'Dreams! youthful dreams!' the priest laughed in mockery.

'You may jeer at us today, Aba Tekle, but one day you may regret it.'

'Why, you are threatening me, Gebreye. Here, you had better slap my cheeks right now,' he jeered at him further. 'You are playing with fire, you young dreamers. Because Dejach Wondirad by some error lost the battle of Chako you feel you are strong enough to challenge the queen. I tell you, she has only been testing your strength so far. If the queen once gets angry and strikes, she strikes hard! Don't be fooled by your chance victory.'

Gebreye, disgusted with the priest's ideas, suddenly stopped eating. 'Just give me a wancha of tella, mother, to wash the food down my throat,' he said to Aberash, wiping his fingers on one end of the enjera.

'But you haven't tasted the chicken or the eggs, son,' she said imploringly. 'There, there. Taste that; it is delicious,' she added, pushing the fleshy leg of a chicken to his side of the traditional tray.

'I have had enough, mother, I just want a wancha of tella.'

'Now, now, you are not going to sit down and watch us while we are feasting, Gebreye. It is not proper manners to stop eating while others are enjoying their food,' Aba Tekle remarked.

'I have no evil eye, don't be afraid of my watching you.'

'Why, are you offended, Gebreye, by chance? Or is there something wrong? You don't seem to be the fine young lad I knew a few years back,' he said, chasing away a fat blue fly which buzzed around his left ear, and darted down to settle on the enjera before him. It instantly took off again, buzzed around his right ear and came down to alight on the enjera before him once more. 'The devil's creature!' Aba Tekle shouted with irritation, waving his fly-switch.

'It's not a devil's creature,' Gebreye contradicted him. 'Only God can create.'

'Yes, yes. It's the devil's creature,' Aba Tekle said, still waving his fly-switch. 'God created the bee. And the devil trying to imitate providence ended up by producing this nuisance.' He laughed aloud at his own joke. Mulatu laughed too. So did Aberash. But Gebreye did not even smile.

The fly took off again, perched on Aba Tekle's immaculate white turban, leaving a reddish stain on it, and buzzed down once again to settle this time on the delicious cooked egg before him.

'The devil take you!' Aba Tekle swore. Rolling the egg in the enjera he neatly slipped it into his mouth. Gebreye felt like vomiting.

Lunch over, Aba Tekle blessed the house once more, and left for his quarters, undoubtedly wounded by Gebreye's unrespectful remarks. As soon as he had gone Mulatu asked his son what had become of him lately. 'I didn't want to say anything in the presence of Aba Tekle, but I am really ashamed of you today. You must go and apologise to him, Gebreye.'

'I am sorry, father. I could judge by your tense face, as well as mother's, that both of you were displeased with my remarks.

86

But I am not going to apologise to Aba Tekle for whatever I said.'

'If you don't, then I will.'

'That's up to you, but I am not going to apologise to him. I detest all priests, who neither toil like the peasants, nor trade like merchants, nor fight like soldiers, but live in idleness throughout their lives, talking nonsense, eating other men's bread, and depending on other people's sweat.'

'Now stop it, son. You came to comfort your father, not to hurt him.'

'I am sorry, father,' Gebreye apologised again. 'I won't say anything more about Aba Tekle from now on, before you.'

'I would very much appreciate that!' Mulatu shouted. 'We had better keep our opinions to ourselves in regard to such matters. We differ so much!'

II

The Battle of Beleha

The rebels were gathered in Kassa's tent discussing the fast
approaching battle over a gembo of honey wine when Gebreye
arrived. His smiling face told them that he had not attended any
funeral at Quara and that his father was well and fine. It was
only out of courtesy that Kassa asked him how his father was
doing. 'He is in perfect health,' Gebreye replied. 'As I suspected
right from the start, mother exaggerated his illness in order to
have an excuse to have me called home.'

'You mean he was not ill in the first place?'

'He was ill, certainly. He was suffering from malaria. But now
he has totally regained his health.'

'What other good news from the district? What do people
say about us?'

'I haven't met many people, Dejazmach; I haven't heard anything bad about us either, except from one royalist who strongly
believes that the old woman of Gondar is going to beat the
pants off us.'

'Who is that royalist?'

'He is not significant enough for you to know him, Dejazmach. He is a priest in our district.'

'A priest?'

'Yes, a priest. He is in fact my father's confessor, and a good
friend of his.'

'And he believes that Woizero Menen is going to beat the pants off us?'

'Regrettably he does. But his opinions and beliefs are not to be given much attention, Dejazmach. I have known the royalist for a long time, since my childhood days, and ever since I have known him I have only once seen him fight for a cause.'

'When was that?'

'Very lately, Dejazmach, the very day I arrived home.'

'What cause was he fighting for?' Kassa was intrigued.

'The cause . . . well, I don't know how to put it. But the cause was really to fill his belly.'

Kassa detected that Gebreye was in a jolly mood. 'I thought you were serious!' he said to him.

'I am serious, Dejazmach. At least I am trying to be.'

'Who was he fighting against?'

'You should ask me what and not who he was fighting against.'

'Then what was he fighting against?'

'He was fighting a fly, Dejazmach, a fat blue fly that kept on perching on his food as we were eating lunch at home last Sunday.'

'Who won in the fight?' Gelmo intervened chuckling, 'the priest or the fly?'

'I should say the fly. It buzzed away triumphantly without a scratch, leaving a stain on the immaculate turban of the royalist!' Gebreye forced a burst of laughter from his friends.

'I will surprise . . . what do they call him?' Kassa wanted to know the name of the royalist.

'Aba Tekle.'

'I will surprise Aba Tekle by making this queen of his grind hot pepper in a cavern. I have been informed that Woizero Menen is going to lead the expedition herself. If the information I have received is correct she is going to mobilise anything between fifteen and twenty thousand soldiers, in other words an army of about seven *negarits*. To win a battle against such a force will not be easy. But we are going to win this battle as we won the battle of Chako. We are going to concentrate on one thing throughout this campaign – on either capturing Menen or killing her as early after the start of the battle as possible.'

This was an old trick applied in traditional warfare. The warriors being undisciplined, and following only one leader, were lost the moment their war lord was captured or killed. Kassa was conscious of this fact and believed that it was the sure way to defeat Woizero Menen.

The actual battle took place in Beleha, a location close to Lake Tana. It was a very fierce one indeed, as the rebels could not apply their chosen tactics easily. They were outnumbered by the enemy to such an extent that it was extremely difficult for them to spot Woizero Menen at the outset of the battle and take her prisoner or kill her, as they had planned. On the other hand the enemy force, twenty thousand strong, inspired by Woizero Menen's presence on the battlefield, attacked the rebels savagely, making them wonder how long they could resist. Among others, Bezabeh met his death soon after Kassa had his trumpet blown as a signal to start the fight. A lance flung by Grazmach Moltot entered his neck by the throat and came out by the nape, killing him in a fraction of a second. Ingida and Gelmo were seriously wounded and had to be carried from the battlefield. Kassa himself received a light wound on the shoulder. He was getting very much concerned about the final outcome of the battle when luck opened Gebreye's eyes and enabled him to spot Woizero Menen from afar, behind a wall of her massive force. Gebreye galloped into the massed warriors, crouching so that his body was like a ball and hiding himself behind his large shield from the rain of spears. When Woizero Menen came into range he shook his spear violently and let it fly at a meteor's speed. The spear sank into Menen's enormous thigh, forcing her to roll off the saddle with a moan. One of her bodyguard raised his arm in a counter-attack and was about to release his lance at Gebreye when Kassa, with a well aimed stroke of his curved sword, cut off his hand at the wrist like a branch from a tree. The fight continued, the rebels gaining ground, and the enemies losing heart. The fight continued until it became known to the majority of Woizero Menen's followers that the queen had been seriously wounded and subsequently captured by the rebels. This news destroyed their morale, and they started to beat a retreat. Soon the battle came to an end.

Normally the man who had saved the day would consider himself a hero. But Gebreye did not. He was not happy, despite the fact that the battle had been won. In a sort of childish way he had always had a contempt for Woizero Menen, and usually referred to her as 'the old woman of Gondar', without realising the power contained in that old woman. He now stiffened when Kassa told him that he was the hero of Beleha, as they were riding back to the camp at the end of the battle. 'Call me anything you like, Dejazmach, but not a hero,' he protested, feeling somewhat mocked at.

'What's the matter with you? I mean what I say.'

'Call me anything, but not a hero, Dejazmach.'

'But why? What's the matter with you?'

'You want to know the truth? The bare truth?'

'Yes, of course.'

'I am ashamed of myself, Dejazmach. Honest to God, I am ashamed of what I have done.'

'But why? I just don't understand you, Gebreye.'

'Because I soiled my spear with a woman's blood. Because I dirtied my spear with the blood of a hag.'

'Nonsense! nonsense! Woizero Menen is worth ten men.'

'No matter how many men she is worth in your eyes, Dejazmach, for me she is an old woman like all other old women. And I shall be ashamed of what I have done today for the rest of my life.'

'Believe me, Gebreye, she is worth ten men. She is in fact a monster, a she-monster, and not the ordinary woman you conceive her to be. And so you are the hero of Beleha.'

No words could convince Gebreye that what he had done was heroic; he had wounded a woman with his spear, and nothing could make him feel proud of this deed. 'What are you intending to do with her anyway, now that she is captured?' he asked Kassa as they were nearing the camp.

'That I really don't know. I only wish you had killed her in the battle.'

'You mean it was not shameful enough for me to have wounded her?'

'That's nonsense, Gebreye. You just don't understand what this woman is worth.'

'So what are you going to do with her now?'

'That's my difficulty, Gebreye. I just don't know. You realise that she is the grandmother of my wife.'

'And so?'

'I'm afraid Tewabech will interfere in this matter. And it will be very difficult for me to ignore whatever she is going to say.'

'She shouldn't interfere, Dejazmach.'

'I only wish she wouldn't.'

Tewabech was in fact impatiently waiting for Kassa to return to their tent in the camp so that she might pour her heart out to him. Throughout the campaign she had felt like the proverbial cow that gave birth to fire and could neither lick it, because it was too hot, nor let it be, because it was her issue. The choice was an impossible one. Tewabech wished that the battle had never been fought in the first place. But the battle had indeed been fought, and her grandmother had been defeated and captured.

What really tortured Tewabech was not the fact of her grand-mother's defeat. The outcome of the showdown was no doubt the better of the two evils. What tortured her was the idea that Kassa might decide to punish her grandmother the way he had punished Dejach Wondirad. The first thing she did, therefore, upon Kassa's entry into their tent was to beg him to forgive Menen. 'Please, my lord,' she entreated him with the deepest feeling, 'please, my lord, don't treat her the way you treated Wondirad. For the sake of our Saviour don't make her suffer an ignoble death.'

'If anyone deserves suffering and death, Woizero Menen deserves it,' he replied with a rising anger

'Please. Please, my lord, for the sake of Christ, our Saviour, give her any punishment you like, but spare her death.'

'No punishment, not even death, is enough for Woizero Menen. You remember, Tewabech, that I came back from the Sudan border with a bullet sunk in my flesh, a bullet that even the best of Quara physicians could not extract, a bullet that I am still carrying in my flesh, and that I shall carry to the end of my days. And Woizero Menen, at whose command and in whose name I had led an expedition, slighted me with her tongue, and sent me, as a further insult, a rotten piece of meat by which to heal my wounds. As if that weren't insult enough, she said, if you remember: "A joint of meat is more than enough for a low-lander." I am a lowlander, and I am not ashamed of it. Why, I might by sheer chance have been born a highlander, but I wouldn't have been any the better on that account. What is most enraging to me in your grandmother is her attitude, her haughtiness, her arrogance, her disdainfulness, her contempt for others. She shall know what being slighted means, now that she is in my hands; she shall know what being humiliated means.'

'Do anything you like, my lord, anything on earth, but spare her life.' Tewabech knelt down before him, pleading on behalf of her grandmother. 'I entreat you in the name of Christ, Our Saviour.'

Kassa suddenly cooled down, as if iced water had been poured on his head. Tewabech's frantic behaviour, the sincerity of her words, her humaneness, and the glistening tears in her eyes, softened him to a point he could hardly have believed himself capable of. Finally, looking into her melting eyes, he said, 'All right, Tewabech. For your sake I shall pardon your grandmother.'

Tewabech was about to fall down and touch his bare feet with her lips in gratitude, when as swift as lightning he lifted her up by the chin and, embracing her, said: 'I can't understand how you could be the granddaughter of this evil woman! I can't understand how the same blood that flows in your veins could also flow in hers!'

Kassa not only spared Woizero Menen's life; he allowed Amede, when he had been called from Quara, to dress her wounds, after he had dressed the wounds of Ingida and Gelmo. On top of that he permitted Tewabech to visit her on certain hours, and to provide her with what she wanted.

Gelmo bitterly criticised Kassa for this undeserved kindness he showed to Woizero Menen, when he had half recovered from his own wound. 'I really don't understand you, Dejazmach,' he said to him as he lay on a leather bed, his forehead thickly bandaged with a brown cotton cloth. 'You treat her like a veritable queen when she deserved nothing less than death, a painful death.'

'I told you Gelmo, a long time ago, that Tewabech would be in my way if I married her. I was not wrong!'

'No, Dejazmach. But Tewabech must choose between you and her family so that your way may be clear.'

'She made her choice the day we got married.'

'On whose side is she?'

'What a question you are asking me, Gelmo. Don't you know whether Tewabech is on our side or not?'

'Don't be angry with me, Dejazmach,' Gelmo sighed. 'I just want to know exactly where she stands.'

'Of course she is on our side. She would sacrifice anything for me, anything in the world, including her life.'

'Why, then, did she beg you to spare Menen's life? Why did she interfere?'

'Certainly not because she loves Menen, or because she is on her side.'

'Then?'

'Because she is human. So much so that if I had had Menen executed she would have died of grief. Besides,' he went on, 'hadn't all this been foreseen before my marriage to her? Didn't I say that she would be a burden to me? And despite my protest, didn't you and Ingida insist that I accept the marriage proposal? Why do you complain about it now?'

'We all insisted on your acceptance of the proposal, Dejazmach. But we also suggested that if Tewabech became a burden to you, you should get rid of her, and clear your way.'

'I don't want to argue with you about this subject any further, Gelmo, because you are still suffering from a wound. But let me tell you one thing, just one thing – that I shall never, never part from Tewabech.' He walked out.

Gelmo turned his bandaged head towards Ingida, who was lying about a yard away from him, and looked at him inquiringly. Ingida answered the inquiry with a silent look of his own. 'He will certainly not divorce her, never,' his look seemed to say, 'for she is an angel. We all know that.'

12

A Hollow Concession

Ras Ali was either a great coward or a very shrewd man. His reaction to the bad news that his mother had been captured was that of a cool peace-seeker. 'We are in-laws,' he reminded Kassa in the verbal message he sent him. 'As such, what happened at Beleha should never have happened between us. Tewabech being our daughter and your beloved wife, we are one through her; I repeat, therefore, that what has happened at Beleha should never have happened between us. Now I would like to apologise on behalf of my mother, who aroused your anger and caused the tragic battle of Beleha. We must quickly put an end to this shameful enmity between in-laws, and re-establish a peaceful union between us. The only condition I require of you to re-establish a peaceful reunion is to release my mother, your mother-in-law, and send her back to Gondar. If you agree to my proposal I promise to make you the governor of Quara and Dembia, with the title of Dejazmach.'

The rebels were expecting Ras Ali to have his war drums beaten and march to Beleha to liberate his captive mother by force. They did not, nevertheless, consider him an outright coward for failing to do so. They rather interpreted his move to mean something else. 'He is as cunning as Woizero Menen herself,' Ingida said, when the rebels met together to discuss what answer should be sent back to Ras Ali. 'He is offering you exactly what you already have – the governorship of Dembia and Quara, with the title of Dejazmach. You are already Dejazmach by popular will, and now that Menen is defeated and captured you are the master of Dembia and Quara. So I see no new concession on the part of Ras Ali.'

'I suppose Ras Ali has nothing else to concede short of his own title and his governorship,' Gelmo put in.

'What do you propose we should do now, in the present situation?' Kassa sought their opinion, though at heart he had already decided for reasons of his own to accept Ras Ali's terms.

'We must march on Debre Tabor and destroy it,' Gebreye blurted out. 'We should not waste any more time.'

'Yes, we must march on Debre Tabor,' Gelmo seconded Gebreye.

A pause followed. It was a deliberate pause. Kassa, sensing the feelings of his fellow-rebels, wanted to cool them down. They were drunk with victory, and they would say and do anything, as a drunkard does when he is under the influence of liquor. 'You don't know what you are saying,' he finally said to them very coolly. 'Our soldiers are exhausted after two successive battles, and they need rest. And don't think it is going to be easy to march on Debre Tabor. It is a long way and very tiring.'

'No matter, Dejazmach,' the impatient Gebreye insisted. 'We must make Ras Ali understand that he is conceding nothing by offering you Quara and Dembia, both of which are under your control now.'

'I am not arguing about that, Gebreye. I absolutely agree with you all that Ras Ali is conceding nothing. At the most he is only recognising my existing governorship of the two districts, and my title. But we must accept his terms of peace just the same, in order to give our soldiers a respite and to gain time to strengthen our force.'

'If Ras Ali's peace terms are accepted, Woizero Menen will be released, I understand.' Ingida raised his voice to be better heard.

'Of course, of course. The main demand in the peace terms is her release,' Kassa replied, over murmuring voices.

'I would object very strongly to her release, Dejazmach. She is too dangerous to be let loose. If you release her today she will attack us again tomorrow. She will not give us a respite, as you suppose.'

'I don't really think so, Ingida. Her pride must be shaken, and her confidence gone, after her humiliating defeat in the last battle.'

Opinions were sharply divided between those who stood for the immediate destruction of Debre Tabor, and the more sober ones who, out of conviction or blind devotion to their master, preferred to accept the peace terms.

The latter were less senior men, whose opinions did not carry much weight as yet in serious decisions like the present one. They were all ambitious young ones who wanted to be noticed by Kassa for the sake of their future advancement. Kassa now used them to overbalance the views of the three who stood strongly for the immediate destruction of Debre Tabor. These three, and especially Gelmo and Ingida, suspected that Tewabech might be influencing Kassa behind the scenes. Perhaps she was taming him, perhaps she was softening him gradually to abandon the cause. No one could blame them for entertaining such a suspicion after her interference in the affair of Woizero Menen, although their suspicion was utterly unfounded. Tewabech was a loving housewife for Kassa. She loved him as much as any wife can love. But she did not influence him so far as to divert the course of his political actions, and in all likelihood she would never try to do so in the future. Politics was not in her veins, despite the fact that she was the granddaughter of the iron-willed Woizero Menen. She was a housewife, a loving housewife and she wanted nothing better than to remain so.

The suspicions of Ingida and Gelmo, however understandable, were therefore utterly unfounded. And Kassa, supported by the majority of his less senior men, stood his ground. He would not decide on the immediate destruction of Debre Tabor.

When the decision was finally taken to accept Ras Ali's peace terms, Woizero Menen was brought to Kassa's audience hall to be informed of the situation.

Kassa imagined that Woizero Menen would rejoice at the news, but that she would at the same time feel crushed by having to stand before him and see him face to face, just as Wondirad had felt crushed after the battle of Chako. But how mistaken Kassa was! Menen was made of harder stuff than Wondirad or any other of her senior officers. When she stood before him, instead of lowering her eyes with shame she held her chin high and defiantly asked him what he wanted of her.

'I have received a message from your son, ma'am,' he said to her politely, 'and I want you to hear it.'

'Whatever message my son has sent you, you remain in my mind what you were before – an ungrateful lowlander, and the son of a kosso-seller.' The warriors around Kassa, the warriors who had gathered to watch the new drama, were dumbfounded, as was Kassa himself. After a second of absolute silence Gebreye tore his way out from the gathering crowd and raised his hand to slap Woizero Menen on the face, a slap that would in all likelihood have cut open her tender skin. But before Gebreye could bring down his arm Kassa shouted at him in anger: 'Stop that, Gebreye. Stop it!'

Gebreye remained for a while in his strange posture, his body thrown back, his right arm in the air, his palm wide open and the heel of one foot a little bit raised from the floor.

'She is a woman like all other women, Gebreye. You know

that as well as I, don't you? And she shall be treated like a woman!' Kassa hissed out between his teeth, his face dark and tense, his eyes flashing in anger. 'Take her out of my sight and give her some work to do,' he ordered. The chief prison guard, who readily understood what his master wanted, took Woizero Menen away and confined her in a solitary cavern. He provided her with a mill and a millstone, and told her to grind red pepper with which to season the soldiers' meals.

For two months Woizero Menen remained in her cavern, labouring like a slave-girl. The soft skin of her palms swelled into blisters of watery fluid, which later burst, letting out the fluid and leaving her palm aching and sore. Towards the end of her confinement the outer skin peeled off, leaving a harder skin behind.

At the end of the two months, when Kassa was assured that Menen's pride was crushed, he set her free, thus formally accepting Ras Ali's peace terms.

13

The Woman of Gondar, II

Woizero Menen returned to Gondar fuming with rage. 'Lord!'
she said, raising her eyes heavenwards, 'what have I done to
you, Lord? What sins have I committed, to deserve this treat-
ment at the hands of my foe? Did you raise me so high, Lord,
only to cast me down so low? Like a slave! He made me grind
red pepper like a slave! No, it was worse than that. A slave does
her work in the clean, open air. My fate was worse than that.
Grinding red pepper in a stinking, suffocating damp cave was
worse than the work of a slave. Why did you raise me so high,
Lord, only to cast me down so low? Why did you not let me
die in the battle of Beleha, Lord?'

Her heart torn with grief and remorse, Woizero Menen returned to Gondar crying out to her Lord for an explanation of
why he had finally abandoned her. The Lord heard her cry, but
gave no explanation.

Woizero Menen soon abandoned Atse Facil castle, the ancient
seat of power, to reside instead in a less imposing house in the
city proper. The castle was in a deteriorating condition and uncomfortable to live in, but Woizero Menen's decision to
abandon it was not based on her wish for a more comfortable
home. If her pride had remained with her she would not have
abandoned the awe-inspiring castle, whatever its condition.
She wished rather to break away from her past. It was too pain-

ful to remember. It hurt her to remember the days when she used to climb to the upper balcony of the castle and watch the human worms moving about, to and from the city proper. After her fall she came to realise that the human worms were not after all worms, and that they were not as small as she had thought them to be, watching them from the balcony of the castle. And this realisation convinced her that it was time she abandoned the ancient seat of power and inhabited a less prominent dwelling.

For two years or so Woizero Menen retired into the shade, and acted only as adviser to her son. During those two years things were quiet, at least on the surface. Kassa Hailu governed Dembia and Quara in peace. Dejach Wube of Tigre paid the usual tribute to the central government and ruled over the northern province without any sign of disturbance. And everything else seemed all right. But this lull did not continue for long. Dejach Goshu of Gojam rebelled against the central government, as he had done several times before, sending a shock wave all over the country. Dejach Goshu was a notorious old warrior who apparently had no ambition to replace Ras Ali as the leader of the country one day, unlike Dejach Wube of Tigre who waited patiently for the chance to come. But Goshu made it clear, time and again, that he wanted hands kept off his province. He remained quiet only as long as there was no interference from outside in the affairs of Gojam province. The moment Ras Ali showed signs of his overlordship, Goshu shook his head and rallied his forces for defence. Several times Ras Ali had tried to catch him. But every time Goshu had slipped away to a mountain fortress called Jibela, to brag from its heights: 'If Ali attempts to climb up, I will let loose the rocks to fall upon his head.'

As it was extremely difficult, if not impossible, to attack Goshu on his mountain, Ras Ali made no attempt to scale its heights. Instead he burnt the villages in the province, punished Goshu's followers and retired to Debre Tabor with the hope that peace would reign, only to discover that peace could not reign in that province. The moment Ali turned his back on Gojam, Goshu descended from his mountain fortress, terrorised the waverers into accepting him as the sole master of the province, and re-established his authority there.

The fresh revolt that broke out now in Gojam, after two years of relative peace in the entire country, was a cause of concern for Ras Ali, who was afraid that it might have far-reaching consequences. A small fire in a forest, if left unchecked, can grow into a conflagration and lay waste an entire district. If the revolt in Gojam was not contained, Ras Ali was afraid that similar revolts would follow in its wake. On the other hand he did not dare to leave Debre Tabor and lead an attack on Gojam, leaving a power vacuum behind him that Kassa would most likely rush to fill. Ras Ali had never had any illusions about the peace terms concluded after the battle of Beleha. He knew that they served only a temporary purpose; that Kassa would make a come-back. And so he was afraid to leave Debre Tabor to quell the fresh rebellion in Gojam. Distressed as he was with the situation he rode to Gondar to consult with his mother about the new development.

Woizero Menen was getting old and weak by this time. She was ageing and physically deteriorating fast, like the weather-beaten castles of Gondar. Her mind, however, was still active; it was as potent as ever.

Woizero Menen listened attentively to her son's woes as she leisurely munched quanta, a snack of dried minced meat much favoured by aristocratic ladies, who rapidly grew fat. 'Of course you will not attack Goshu,' she finally said to him in a cool tone of voice.

'Then?'

'You will promise him the governorship of Quara in addition to his governorship of Gojam, provided that he turns the lance he aimed at you on the rebel, Kassa.'

Ras Ali stared at his mother in stupefaction and asked her whether she genuinely believed that Goshu was stronger than Kassa, and whether, first of all, Goshu would accept such a proposal.

'The question is not whether Goshu is stronger than Kassa, or Kassa stronger than Goshu, my son,' she said to him, still in a cool tone of voice. 'The main thing is that the one should fight against the other, and both leave you alone. They won't let you govern the country in peace, Ali,' she went on, with pain and remorse in her voice. 'They are wolves; you can maintain your grip on the country only by playing off the one against the other.'

'But supposing that Goshu turns down the proposal because he is afraid to attack Kassa, what would be the outcome of the scheme? Wouldn't I be making myself the target of two bloodthirsty hounds at the same time?'

'You underestimate Goshu because of his age, Ali. I am sure that his heart is still young. He will not hesitate for a second before falling on Kassa like a hound, once he is assured of augmenting his territory by such a large district as Quara. If he were the coward or the weak old man you imagine him to be he would not, in the first place, have defied your overlordship.'

'But supposing that he does decline the proposal?'

'What if he does? You will not be losing a friend in him, will you? And I suppose you don't consider Kassa to be one of your faithful generals, either?'

'I have never had that illusion.'

'Then you have to take the risk, son. If Goshu turns down your offer we shall consider what action you should take. The first thing is to find out what his reaction is.'

Woizero Menen was not mistaken in believing that her scheme would work. No sooner had Goshu received the proposal than he accepted it in full, and no sooner had he accepted it than he sent a bold message to Kassa telling him either to relinquish his claim over Quara in peace, or to make ready for an inevitable battle between them. Goshu was young in heart, indeed!

14

More City Gossip, and the Battle of Guramba

When the matter became public the Gondares had their usual gossip over it.

'He is acting the sacrificial lamb.'

'Who?'

'Dejach Goshu, of course.'

'Who is sacrificing him?'

'Ras Ali and his mother.'

'You mean he cannot stand against Kassa?'

'Have you ever seen an old bull stand against a robust young one?'

'This is not a man-to-man fight.'

'No matter. Goshu cannot hope to win a battle against a man who captured and degraded the queen herself.'

'Goshu almost succeeded in making Gojam independent. At no time has Ras Ali totally subjugated him.'

'Well, let them fight it out. We shall see who will be the victor.'

Kassa Hailu was very unhappy to receive Goshu's challenge. Goshu either underestimated him, or overestimated himself. 'This old man Goshu must have lost his power of reasoning,' Kassa said to his inner circle the day the challenge reached him. 'Otherwise he would have known that he doesn't stand the slightest chance of winning.'

'What could have prompted him to take such a foolish decision, Dejazmach?' Ingida asked.

'It's an open secret that it was Woizero Menen's idea to divert his action towards me. It's a pity that Dejach Goshu has no adviser to dissuade him from attempting the impossible. He is like the proverbial bull which broke its neck trying to reach the greenery at the bottom of an abyss. He wants to add Quara to his province, and does not see the possibility of losing Gojam altogether! He still thinks Kassa is the runaway of old times, a poor orphan without a home or a family. I tell you, Goshu has lost his power of reasoning.'

'But Dejazmach,' Ingida went on to ask, 'do you believe that Woizero Menen has really promised him the governorship of Quara? Is it not just a rumour?'

'A rumour? It's not a rumour, Ingida, it's a fact.'

'But you have been sending tribute to the government in Gondar for the last two years, and you have shown no disloyalty to the regime in all that time. Why should they provoke you to arms once again?'

'You forget one thing. Woizero Menen has received a wound in her pride that will never heal; and she would go to any lengths to avenge herself. When people lose their pride, their self-esteem, they will do anything in their power to restore that lost pride. They retire to some obscure corner where they can't be seen, where they can't be heard, where they can't be mocked. There in their shade, in their underground, they prepare some poison to avenge themselves not only against their personal foes but against the world, against the innocent as well as the guilty. But that's beside the point. What Woizero Menen is trying to do is to kill two birds with one stone – to put an end to the rebellion in Gojam, and weaken whichever of us comes out victorious in the inevitable battle.'

'If that is her intention, Dejazmach, why not disappoint her by making terms with Dejach Goshu, and jointly attacking Ras Ali?' This was Gelmo's suggestion.

'No, we are not going to do that,' Kassa replied decisively. 'However wise your suggestion may be, Gelmo, I cannot dishonour myself by not accepting Goshu's challenge. What we are going to do is crush Goshu, and march on Debre Tabor immediately after.'

'We have already waited too long, Dejazmach.' Gebreye was happy at Kassa's decision. 'We should have marched on Debre Tabor immediately after the battle of Beleha.'

'Perhaps you are right, Gebreye, perhaps you are right.'

In the brief battle that ensued the rugged Gojames proved to be as tough as ever. They were very good lancers and excellent shots in addition to being superb horsemen. Kassa could not believe his eyes when he saw, in the battle of Guramba, some of his followers retreating, terrified by the ruthless butchery of the Gojames. He himself, under a shower of shots, was forced to retreat into a maize plantation. Dejach Goshu, spotting him from a distance, followed him into the plantation. Kassa took cover behind his black charger, set his musket on the saddle of his horse to steady his aim, and when Goshu came into range, galloping and splitting the air with his war-cry, he let off a ball that cracked Goshu's head open instantly, and tore out his brain, scattering bits of it in the wind. Kassa rushed on his fallen foe, picked up his blood-drenched toga and, hoisting it like a flag on the tip of his lance, galloped towards the enemy force, shouting at the top of his voice: 'Here is your leader! Here is Goshu!'

The Gojames, panic-stricken, started to cast away their shields and spears, admitting defeat. Victory once again went to the 'rebel'.

15

End of an Era

Kassa Hailu did not waste any more time before getting ready for the most decisive battle he had ever fought in his life. The battle of Chako, the battle of Beleha and the battle of Guramba were simple military exercises compared to the one that was to follow, for its outcome was to decide the fate not only of two men – Ras Ali of Yeju, and Kassa Hailu of Quara – but of the entire country. Victory for Ras Ali would mean the maintainance of the status quo, while that of Kassa would herald a change, and a drastic one. Kassa's defeat would only entail the end of a rebellion in the western section of the central province, while Ras Ali's would put an end to the succession of the Yeju dynasty, and open up a new era.

Seeing the importance and decisiveness of the fast-approaching conflict neither Ras Ali nor Dejach Kassa spared any effort in mobilising the largest possible army. Kassa's, which had been augmented by defectors, admirers and adventurers after each victorious battle, was certainly a power to reckon with. And yet compared to the army Ras Ali could mobilise it was a drop of water to a bucketfull.

Ras Ali, apart from his own followers – who were by themselves several times more numerous than Kassa's – mobilised the entire force that was once commanded by his mother. In addition he ordered Dejach Wube of Tigre to send him a contingent headed by a major, which he did immediately. Armed with cannon, matchlocks and traditional weapons Ras Ali's force, nearly a hundred thousand strong, intercepted Kassa before Kassa could reach Debre Tabor. Looking through a pair of binoculars that a certain Englishman had given him as a present, Ras Ali surveyed Kassa's men from far off. Finding them unimpressive he observed: 'They are too many to be guests for a wedding party, and yet too few to deserve the name of an army.' Kassa, on the other hand, after surveying Ras Ali's force with his naked eyes turned to his followers and observed: 'I still believe that it takes a ball of iron to smash fifty clay jars.'

Soon after this, cannons boomed out in Aisha, the location of the battle. Balls zoomed through the air, tearing away bits of live flesh from those of both sides. Spears and lances flashed in the sun before sinking into the body of one unfortunate warrior or another.

Ras Ali saw heads chopped off the shoulders of his men, limbs torn from their bodies and eyes dug out of their sockets. His men fought bravely. They advanced like waves, mad waves, towards the enemy and crashed against them as waves crash against the rocky shores of the sea, only to recede leaving a mass of dead flesh behind them – a heap of chopped-off heads and torn-off limbs.

'This is a curse from God!' Ras Ali was forced to say, astonished by the enemy's dexterity in handling weapons and manipulating the reins of their supple horses. 'I thought I was fighting a man, but in truth I am fighting the devil incarnate. I give up,' he cried. Spurring his horse, he galloped away from the battlefield towards Yeju, his fatherland, to save his life from the wrath of the enemy.

Ras Ali's flight marked the end of one era and the beginning of another. Kassa Hailu was now seeing the beginning of the fulfilment of the prophecy. And so leaping off his horse he knelt down and prayed in silence, thanking his creator for enabling him to advance the cause so far.

16

The Drunken Soldier
and the Cat-eyed Ferengi

In the evening, when the conquering army was feasting, as was its custom, on reeking raw meat and hard liquor, a half-drunk soldier staggered out from among the throng and came to stand before Kassa. 'I've zeen a ztrange creater vighting beside ze enemy, Deyazmach,' he said, letting his lower jaw hang down.

'What did he look like?' Kassa queried, laughing good-humouredly at the drunken soldier.

'His faze waz like a red bebber, Deyazmach, an' his 'air was like a monkey's fur.'

'You're totally drunk, soldier.'

'I am not drunk, Deyazmach. I've zeen such a creater.'

'His face must have been covered with blood if he looked like a red pepper, soldier, and he could have been wearing a fur cap.'

'He was not zcratched, Deyazmach, an' his 'ead was bare.'

'He is talking of the cat-eyed Ferengi,' another soldier intervened. 'I saw him myself on the battlefield.'

'You did?'

'Yes, Dejazmach.'

'Has anyone else seen the white man?'

Many people answered in the affirmative.

'Was he killed?'

'I don't know, Dejazmach,' the second soldier replied.

Kassa summoned Gebreye and instructed him to find out the whereabouts of the stranger. Gebreye in turn called several soldiers and sent them to different areas of the camp. It didn't take long to discover the whereabouts of the white man, since he was among the captives taken that day. Before the feast was over he was brought to the feasting-place. He was dressed like an ordinary Ethiopian warrior, his attire consisting of a pair of trousers that reached a little below the knees, a long shirt and a white toga over the shirt. His face was in fact red, as the drunkard had described it, a dull red. One could have easily taken him for a fair-coloured Ethiopian, if it had not been for his blue eyes and his soft European hair.

'Who are you?' Kassa asked him, through an interpreter called Samuel.

'John Bell,' he answered.

'From what country?'

'From England. I am the subject of Her Majesty Queen Victoria.'

'Why did you come to my country? Has your queen sent you on government affairs?'

'I came on my own desire, Dejazmach. My country has nothing to do with my presence in your country.'

Kassa suspected John Bell was lying, and went on to ask him again why he came to Ethiopia.

'I came because I had heard of your country, of its good climate, of its dense forests, of its . . .'

'Doesn't the sun shine in your country?' Kassa interrupted him.

'It does.'

'Doesn't it rain in your country at all?'

'It does.'

'Why then did you come to my country if, as you say, the sun also shines in yours, and the rain falls also in yours?'

John Bell tried to explain the difference between the English climate and a tropical one. But the explanation did not fully satisfy Kassa. He still suspected that John Bell had something else in mind in coming to Africa.

'You haven't said anything about my people. Do you like them too, as you like the sunshine of my country?'

'I like the ones who are kind to me.'

'And the ones who are not kind to you?'

'I don't like them.'

'He must be an honest man to say that,' Kassa observed, turning to Ingida and Gebreye who were beside him. But these two were more suspicious of the Ferengi than Kassa himself.

'Do you still want to stay in my country? Or now that your master, Ali, as fled to Yeju do you want to go back to your own country?'

'I should very much like to stay here, Dejazmach, if you would allow me to do so.'

'I will certainly allow you to stay, on two conditions. First of all, you will try to open up communication between your queen and myself; secondly, since you are a soldier, you will train my men in the art of European warfare.'

'I will try to do the second, but I am afraid the first is beyond my power.'

'I say you will try to open up communication between your queen and myself. This you must do if you want to stay.'

'I was not sent here by my queen, Dejazmach. And so I cannot directly open communication between you and our queen. But I can contact our queen's envoy, who is in Massawa, and who can open up communication between you and our queen. I understand that the envoy had already signed a treaty with Ras Ali and that he knows your country well.'

'A treaty signed by Ras Ali will not be binding on me. But I want the friendship of your queen just the same. And so you will inform the envoy as early as you can about my desire to be a friend of the queen. What is his name, by the way?'

'Plowden. Walter Chichile Plowden.'

'Good. You will contact Ato Plowden as soon as you can. Now you can go.' Kassa dismissed John Bell, giving strict orders to his followers that he was to be treated kindly as a guest and not as a captive. He also gave him permission to travel freely in the country and to hunt in the wild forest if he was so disposed.

17

An Angel Tormented

Kassa retired to his private tent very late at night to find Tewabech alone, sitting motionless behind the flickering light of a kerosene lamp. She was silent and sad, but calm. Throughout the evening, while the soldiers as well as the servants were celebrating the victory of Aisha, she had remained alone, mourning the fate of her father.

Kassa walked straight to his bed without uttering a word, undressed himself down to his waist in the dim light of the lamp, and lay down on the bed. He knew, of course, why Tewabech was so silent and so sad. He felt pressed to talk to her, at least to say something, but he was at a loss how and where to start. He twisted and turned about on the leather bed for some time. Then when the silence became too heavy, unbearably heavy, he gathered his strength and called out her name. She remained silent, silent as the grave. 'Tewabech!' he called out again, loud, as if she were miles away from him, as indeed she was in spirit. She started and said: 'Wei.'

'I had no choice in doing what I have done, Tewabech, you must understand.'

'I haven't blamed you for anything, my lord.'

'Forgive me, Tewabech, forgive me for Heaven's sake.'

'Forgive you for what, my lord?'

'For my sin, for my unpardonable sin.'

'Sin? You haven't committed any sin, you have only done what you had to do.'

'Why, then, are you so cross with me?'

'I am not cross with you, my lord, only I have to bear my burden. It's Christ's will that I should suffer.'

'Supposing that I had lost the battle, would you have been happier, Tewabech? Tell me the truth.'

'My burden would have been heavier; I would have suffered more. I don't understand why God has condemned me to suffer one way or the other. I must have sinned greatly.'

'I had no personal dislike towards your father, Tewabech. I swear to God I had none.'

'But you killed him all the same.'

'What? What are you talking about?'

'I say you killed him just the same.'

'Whoever told you that is a liar. Your father is alive, not dead.'

'You are not telling me the truth, my lord, are you?'

'I swear to God your father was not even scratched during the fight. He fled to Yeju rather than be captured.'

Tewabech had not believed the story when she heard it from one of her maids, who in turn had heard it from one of the soldiers earlier in the evening. Now she felt greatly relieved, for Kassa would not have sworn on God if he had been telling her a lie.

Tewabech sank back into her silence for a moment and then asked Kassa what he would have done to her father if he had been captured during the battle.

'Before I answer that question I beg you to leave that stool, and come over here.'

'Answer me first. Would you have had him killed?'

'If I wanted to have anyone killed it would be your grandmother, not Ras Ali. Believe me, Tewabech, I had no personal dislike towards him.'

Tewabech left her stool and came to sit on the edge of the leather bed. 'What would you have done to my father if he hadn't escaped?' she insisted.

'I would have had him put in custody until the situation became calm and stable. Then I would have released him for your sake, if not for anything else. What did I do, after all, to Woizero Menen after the battle of Beleha?'

'Don't talk about her, my Lord, she is at the root of all evil. I hate her from the bottom of my heart.'

'You are not going to bear me a grudge on account of your father, Tewabech, are you?'

Tewabech declined to answer the question, she remained silent. But her hand was now unconsciously, as it were, caressing the broad hairy chest of her husband.

'I regret the fate of your father, Tewabech, but I couldn't really help doing what I did.'

Tewabech refrained from making any comment; she just went on caressing his chest dreamily. There was still sadness in her face, a serene sadness. But behind the sadness there was, too, a glimmer of joy. Kassa looked at her intently for a long time, fascinated by that intermittent glow in her face, by that mingled sorrow and joy in her soul, until he pressed her against his chest, suddenly overcome by passion.

18

Mission to the North

A few weeks after the battle of Aisha, Kassa had Samuel, his secretary interpreter, called to his tent to tell him of his intention to send him on a very important mission to the northern province of Tigre. Considering the importance of the mission he had in mind, Kassa would have liked to send Gebreye or another of his senior men, if circumstances had allowed him to do so. But he could not send any of his senior men because, a fresh rebellion having broken out in Gojam, he was preparing to leave for the southern province; and so he was not in a position to lose Gebreye or any of the other warriors. Besides, there was probably no person better able than Samuel to carry out this particular mission, as Samuel was born in the northern province and knew it inside out. In addition, Samuel was well acquainted with the men to whom the message was to be directed.

'You told me some time ago that you knew Dejach Wube quite well, right?' Kassa asked Samuel as the latter stood respectfully before him.

'Yes, Dejazmach. I know Dejach Wube very well. My father was a chief in Senafe, and every year when he went to see Dejach Wube, to hand over the tax he had collected from the peasants, I used to accompany him to Aduwa. Of course it is a very long time now since I saw Dejach Wube, but still I remember his face as though I saw him only yester-day.'

'Good, good, Samuel. Now I want to send you to Dejach Wube with a message of the utmost importance.'

'It will be an honour for me, Dejazmach.'

'Go and tell him, tell Dejach Wube, that Kassa wants no more bloodshed; tell him that he, Wube, shall remain the governor of Tigre and Semen despite the active participation of his troops in the last battle against me, and despite the changes that have occurred recently in Gondar, provided that he accepts my overlordship in peace, and lets Aba Selama, the bishop, come to Gondar. Tell him further that if he does not accept these terms there will be war between us, a war that I shall deplore if it ever comes to pass.'

'Yes, Dejazmach.'

'That is not all, Samuel. Whatever reply you get from Dejach Wube, you will then proceed to see Aba Selama in per-son and tell him that I am inviting him to come to Gondar. Tell him further that it is in his own interest and in the interest of the Orthodox Church that I am inviting him to come.'

'Yes, Dejazmach.'

'And I want you to bring me an answer from both by the time I return from the Gojam expedition.'

Samuel elaborately bowed down in agreement and re-tired.

It was only recently that Samuel had come into the service of Kassa, only a few weeks before the battle of Aisha. Samuel was not a warrior, and had neither the ambition nor the in-clination to become one. However, he sympathised with the rebels' cause and supported it with all his heart.

Samuel was a young man of about twenty-eight. He had gone abroad when he was about sixteen, and had studied history and languages. He had lived in Egypt for some time, and then in

India where he learnt a great deal about England and France, the major world powers of the time. Upon his return home Samuel could hardly find a job, as the age required men with sturdy, muscular arms and calves, men who could wield the spear and manipulate a horse, not sickly-looking young men like Samuel whose main interest in life was reading history and acquiring knowledge. And so his education and his extensive experience abroad would most likely have been wasted in the unsophisticated society of the time if by a piece of good luck he had not come across Kassa.

Even Kassa was not impressed by the meagre look of Samuel when he met him the first time, but he was intrigued by the fact that Samuel had lived abroad and knew the white men more intimately than any of his compatriots did.

'What is it that profited you most in your travels abroad?' he asked him the very first day they met.

'The knowledge of the white man, Dejazmach.'

'In what sense did that profit you?'

'In the sense that there is much one can learn from the white man, but that one should never trust the white man.'

'Never trust a white man? Why do you say that?'

'It's what I saw and observed in India, and what I read in books, that makes me believe that the white man is not to be trusted. Of course I am not talking of individual white men, Dejazmach. There are good and bad white men as there are good and bad black men. When I say that the white man is not to be trusted I mean the white man in general, and the government of the white man in particular.'

'What is it that you observed in India and read in books that makes you hold such a low opinion of the white man and the white man's government?'

'Well, the Indians, for instance, no longer have a country, Dejazmach. The white man took it. That's one thing I know.'

'Why, are all the Indians women? Can't they gird their loins and fight against the white man?'

'If the Indians had known the white man's intentions initially they might have tried to keep them out of their country. But they were duped by the white man, Dejazmach, and that's why I say the white man is not to be trusted.'

'How did the white men come to India, anyway?'

'As friends, Dejazmach. First came the white traders and missionaries; then the councils; and finally, the battalions.'

'Shame! the white man did indeed dupe the Indians. As for me, I would rather deal first with the battalions, then with the missionaries!'

Kassa took a liking for Samuel that first day, when they met and talked about Samuel's experiences abroad. And although Kassa knew that Samuel had no prospect of ever becoming a warrior he took him into his service, aware that he would serve him in a way no warrior could. He therefore entrusted him now with the message to Dejach Wube while he himself headed south to quell the rebellion in Gojam.

19

Beru Goshu, the Counter-Rebel

The rugged Gojamés, from time immemorial, had proved to be an indomitable people who would allow no one to put a yoke on their necks. No sooner were they subdued by one power or another than they raised their arms in rebellion and shook the yoke off their neck like a young unbroken bull. The battle of Guramba in which Kassa killed Goshu, his old-time foe, was not therefore to be the last in which he was to confront the Gojamés.

The leader of the revolt this time was Beru, the son of the late Goshu, who it seems had two motives behind his rebellion, namely to avenge the death of his father and to maintain the independence of the province. The young Beru was, however, very rash in his undertaking, for his army was no match for the now formidable might of Kassa Hailu. The battle that ensued was, therefore, ill-balanced and devoid of drama. Beru was captured after a brief battle, and brought before Kassa with a stone on his nape as a symbol of total submission.

'Throw away the stone on your neck, and come and sit by my side,' Kassa invited Beru. When Beru was unwillingly seated beside him Kassa asked him why he rebelled. Surprised by the apparent naïveté of the question, Beru refused to reply.

'Why did you rebel against me, Beru? Don't you know what

ve are trying to do, all my followers and myself?' he asked him again in a more serious tone.

Beru, suddenly possessed by hatred, cried: 'Because you murdered my father!'

'Murdered your father? You are accusing me of a grave crime, a crime I have not committed.'

'Who, then, murdered my father?'

'No one did.'

'I was there on the battlefield, galloping behind my father, when you cracked open his head and scattered bits of his brain to the wind.'

'And yet, my friend, I didn't murder your father. I only killed him; I assure you that if he had been a little faster in action he would have been alive now, and I in the grave. So much for your father. The next thing I want to know is this. If I had been the captured and you the captor in today's battle, what fate would you have given me, Beru?'

Beru still preferred to remain silent.

'When I ask you a question I expect a prompt reply,' Kassa said to him with a frown. But Beru still gave no answer.

'Speak up.'

Kassa's entourage became restless, and tried to urge Beru to talk.

'What use would it be to you to know that, since it is you who are the captor, and I the captive?'

'Curiosity, my friend. I just want to satisfy my curiosity. Besides, your fate may depend to a large extent on your reply.'

'I refuse to answer the question. I am at your mercy, and you may do what you want to do with me. If you think I am scared of death I assure you I am not.'

'Your refusal, if you persist in it, will not lead you to a happy death, but to a painful existence.'

Beru was indeed unafraid of being put to death. He expected

it, and was ready for it. But he dreaded any kind of torture. He suddenly remembered that Kassa liked playing cat and mouse with his victims. When a cat catches a mouse it does not devour it all at once. It dances around its victim, picks it up between its teeth and lets it drop to the ground. Then it licks its whiskers and starts dancing again around its victim. It pounces on it with its paw, retreats a little, and swoops down upon it once more. Only when the victim is dead does it start mangling its flesh between its teeth. Kassa indeed liked playing cat and mouse with his captured enemies, and Beru, dreading any torture of the kind Dejach Wondirad had undergone, decided to talk. 'So you want my sincere answer?' he said to him finally.

'Yes, of course, your sincere and honest answer,' Kassa replied.

Beru reflected for a moment and said viciously: 'If I had been the victor, if the gracious Lord had allowed me that great honour, I would have had your head chopped off.'

'What?' Kassa jerked back in horror.

'I would have had your head chopped off,' Beru repeated in all sincerity.

A number of soldiers jerked out their curved swords from their scabbards at this dangerous confession. Before they could bring their swords down on Beru's neck, however, Kassa stopped them with a wave of the hand. He said to Gelmo, his brow knitted with anger, 'Take him away from my sight. He is vicious. But I spare him his life just the same for telling me the truth. Tomorrow, send him to Sar Amba where he shall stay with Woizero Menen and the other prisoners for the rest of his life.'

Kassa did not stay long in Gojam after that. Appointing a certain Tedla Gualu, a native of Gojam, as the new governor of the province he made his way back to Gondar with the expecta- tion that Samuel would be back from the mission with a posi- tive answer from Dejach Wube.

20

Fruit of a Forbidden Love

Dejach Wube was the illegitimate son of a Tigrean prince. He was religious by nature, conservative in thought, aristocratic in taste, and unhurried in action. He was happy to live in relative peace, paying a nominal tribute to the now fallen regime of Ras Ali, until such time as conditions were ripe for him to knock down Yeju Galla, the guardian of Emperor Yohannes, and put the time-honoured crown on his own head.

When Dejach Wube had had a new church built in Debre Sege, not so long before, nobody except a few of his closest followers suspected the true motive behind it. It was taken for granted that as he was a pious man he just wanted to add one more to the scores of existing houses of God in Tigre. When through long years of laborious correspondence he finally succeeded in securing a bishop from Alexandria against payment of a large sum of money to Egypt, after the Holy See of St Mark had been vacant for nearly fourteen years, it was again believed by the public that Dejach Wube's only motive was to secure a shepherd for the religious fold. Only the minute section of his inner circle, although not daring enough to discuss the matter openly, suspected, and rightly, that there was something hidden behind the scheme.

If any provincial governor of the period understood the mentality of the Ethiopian people that governor was Dejach

Wube. He knew that the only sure way of governing the unruly masses of northern Ethiopia was through the Church, which for centuries past had moulded the thinking of the Christian populace, making it either obey the secular government or revolt against it according to whether or not the government was favourable to the Church and its innumerable servants priests, debteras (scribes), monks and deacons. As the secular rulers depended on their swords to attain or to maintain power, so did the churchmen on their power of excommunication. 'Anyone who follows so-and-so shall produce a black dog for a child,' the bishop would swear if dissatisfied with a ruler. 'He shall have no place in the church cemetery for his body to rest in; and his soul shall burn in the everlasting fires of hell.' And the people would not dare obey a ruler thus abhorred by, and alienated from the Church.

Dejach Wube, deeply aware of the power and influence of the Ethiopian Orthodox Church, had but to befriend it in order to fulfil his great ambition of one day occupying the 'Throne of David'. Thus, his ultimate motive in adding one more church to the existing ones in Debre Sege, and in importing an Egyptian bishop from Alexandria, was as much, if not more, political than religious.

Dejach Wube had been preparing himself for years past now to oust the Yeju dynasty and to crown himself emperor of Ethiopia. But alas, he waited too long; he was too slow in his proceedings, thus allowing Kassa unexpectedly to steal the show.

It was injury enough for the old, slow aristocrat to hear that an upstart named Kassa had become the ruler of the central province, that vast expanse of land that stretched west of the Tekeze river. But to receive a message from that very man he greatly despised at heart, a threatening message that offered him only the choice between silent submission or a fight, was indeed adding insult to injury.

Dejach Wube was in his private residence (in a new camp he had had built in Semen, in preference to the town of Aduwa), whiling away the time with his charming young daughter, when Samuel was announced. The name Samuel was not unfamiliar to his ears. He remembered the son of one of his minor chiefs in Senafe who bore that name. But he could not make out what the devil that same Samuel could have been doing in Gondar, or how he could have come into the services of the upstart he despised. On reflection, however, he imagined that this must be another Samuel, not the one he had known at Senafe. And unwillingly he left his dimpled, twelve-year-old daughter, and made his way to his audience hall, followed by his shield-bearer, in order to receive Kassa's message.

The audience hall was kept warm by a big crackling fire that sent out sparks in all directions from its centre. The hall was bare of furniture except for half a dozen or so unimposing stools that stood scattered on the bare earth floor. The only colourful objects on the ground were a Turkish carpet that covered the medeb, the raised floor, and a Turkish cushion on it.

In contrast to the nearly bare floor the walls of the audience hall were decorated with glittering spears and shields, as well as a large number of trophies from hunting expeditions. Like so many aristocratic gentlemen of the period, Dejach Wube went to the jungle from time to time to shoot wild animals for pleasure. Most of the trophies in the hall, including the tusk of an elephant and a lion's skin, were his own.

Dejach Wube allowed Samuel to be admitted as soon as he was comfortably seated on the Turkish carpet and leaning against the gaudy-coloured cushion. To his great disappointment Kassa's 'ambassador' was the Samuel he knew, the son of the Senafe chief. He felt jealous that Samuel, ignoring his father's good example of serving him, Dejach Wube, had gone over to the upstart. Aroused by this jealousy, he felt like repri-manding the young man, but containing his emotion he asked him instead what exactly he had come for. Samuel delivered the brief message from Kassa and received as brief an answer: 'Tell your master that Wube is ready to face Kassa any time, any-where.'

'But sir,' said the startled Samuel, who felt that Wube was unaware of Kassa's power, 'Dejach Kassa does not expect such an answer.'

'He doesn't?'

'I assure you, sir, that Dejach Kassa wants no more blood-shed.'

'Of course not! So I shall prove to him to be a coward.'

'But, sir, are you aware of his might?'

'What do you know about him, young man? How long have you been in his service?'

'I have been in his service only recently, sir, but I do know much about him. I know the depths from which he started his career, and I also know the heights to which he has ascended.'

'That he was a nonentity yesterday, and that today he is the governor of the central province?'

Samuel kept silent for a while.

'Go and tell him my reply,' Dejach Wube commanded.

'You should weigh the matter over, sir, before giving him such a reply. Dejach Kassa wants no more bloodshed.'

'You are Kassa's messenger, young man; so act like one. Your mission here is not to be my adviser, but to deliver your master's words and take back my reply. Now you are dis-missed.'

Dejach Wube was not in the least perturbed by Kassa's threat, for he had been expecting it to come sooner or later, and his decision to fight Kassa had been made the day his defeated troops returned from the battle of Aisha.

The next morning Dejach Wube called an urgent meeting of his officers to explain the situation to them. 'I received an ultimatum from Kassa either to submit to him, or to prepare for a showdown,' he said to them.

'If we have to —'

'There are no ifs,' cut in Wube. 'I have already sent Kassa a message informing him that I am ready to face him any time, anywhere.'

'What I was about to say, Dejazmach, is that if we have to fight the sooner we engage him the better for us,' the officer he had interrupted said. 'His men must be exhausted because of their incessant marches and battles. Their morale may still be high because of their various victories, but whether they admit it to themselves or not they must be physically worn out.'

Other officers spoke in approval, and after they had decided where they should wait for the enemy the meeting came to an end.

21

The Romantic Bishop

Samuel's mission to Tigre was not over when he was un-
ceremoniously dismissed from Dejach Wube's audience hall.
Greatly concerned for the unavoidable bloodshed that was to
come, he made his way to Aduwa to meet the bishop.

Aba Selama, the one hundred and eighteenth bishop to come
to Ethiopia from Alexandria, was very young in age. Neither
his long, abundant beard that reminded one of the ancient
apostles, nor his long, wide cassock could hide his youthfulness,
and the inner sensualism of his nature. This sensualism was
particularly accentuated in his sharp sparkling eyes and his
small fleshy lips. Rumour had it that the young bishop was very
romantic indeed, and that he had not less than nine lovers, two
of whom were nuns.

There was, of course, no way of verifying this rumour. It
could have been fabricated by those who did not like the bishop
and who consequently wanted to defame and scandalise him.
On the other hand, judging by his youthfulness and by the
shape of his lips, which gave the impression that they could not
be quenched by any amount of love, the bishop might well
have had one or two lovers, if not nine.

Aba Selama very often stated that he had been brought to
Ethiopia to preach the word of God, and not to do anything
else. By this he meant that politics was outside his domain. But

in fact he spent a good amount of his time in political intrigues. He was fully aware of his key position as a kingmaker, and of the fact that all the ambitious Rasses and Dejazmaches were going on all fours to bring him over to their side. He took full advantage of this situation to advance the cause of the Orthodox Church and its devoted servants.

Now, when Samuel was announced, the bishop was discussing an important matter with Aba Tekle of Quara, the father confessor of Mulatu who had once fallen out with Gebreye because of the insulting remarks he made about Kassa and his fellow rebels. Aba Tekle was afraid of what might ensue in his district after the fall of Ras Ali and Woizero Menen, whom he openly supported. Remembering the rebels' apparently 'anti-Church' attitude, exemplified by Gebreye's argument, he came to Aduwa to meet the young bishop and discuss with him what course of action should be taken in case the rebels attacked the Church by word of mouth, or by action. The discussion between the bishop and the priest being over, the priest could have been excused, but Aba Selama told him to stay and listen to Kassa's message.

The bishop, after allowing Samuel to kiss the golden Coptic cross in his hand, asked him what the content of the message was. Samuel delivered the brief message; that Dejach Kassa was inviting him to come to Gondar.

The purpose of the invitation being quite clear to him, Aba Selama diplomatically tried to decline the invitation, and hastened to explain to Samuel that he was not in good enough health to travel anywhere, and least of all to a distant place like Gondar.

Nonetheless, no soul in the entire country looked healthier than Aba Selama at that time; so Samuel, totally unconvinced of the bishop's lame excuse, said to him boldly: 'The consequences will be grave, your grace, if you decline Dejach Kassa's invitation.' Samuel's words pricked Aba Selama like so many needles. 'Are you threatening me, young man?' he exclaimed, and looked at Aba Tekle's face to read his reaction. Indeed there was an expression of surprise in Aba Tekle's face, too, because of the manner in which Samuel had spoken to the bishop.

'I apologise if I made my statement sound like a threat, your grace; I only meant to state bluntly what will happen if you do decline the invitation.'

'You are talking of consequences, young man. And so your statement remains a threat.'

'Well, if you take it that way there is nothing I can do about it, your grace. But let me remind you that you are not the only bishop residing in this country. And so your refusal to see Dejach Kassa will surely lead to undesirable consequences.'

'What do you exactly mean by that?' the bishop said angrily, his long black beard fluttering.

'I mean there is also Bishop Jacobis in this country.'

'Jacobis, the Jesuit?' Aba Selama exclaimed furiously.

'Yes, your grace,' answered Samuel coolly. 'If you don't cooperate with Dejach Kassa he may resort to the papist, or the Jesuit as you called him. He has in fact approached him already and the Catholic bishop is more than willing to do whatever Dejazmach commands him to do.'

'What a farce!' Aba Selama cried out still more furiously. 'Doesn't your Dejazmach know that I can excommunicate him from the Church if he starts flirting with the Roman bishop?' Again he looked at Aba Tekle's face to read his reaction. The latter nodded vigorously, approving Aba Selama's counter-threat.

'But your grace,' said Samuel reverently, 'if you excommunicate him, Bishop Jacobis will only be too willing to absolve him. And think of the chaos that will ensue as a result.

The Orthodox Church, our Church, is already divided into factions – those who believe in the three births of Christ, those who believe in the two births and those who call themselves the Sons of Grace. If you are going to force Dejach Kassa to favour Bishop Jacobis, the fissure that already exists in the Church will only get wider, and shake the throne of St Mark to its very foundation.'

'I appreciate your knowledge and concern for our Church, young man, but I cannot accept Kassa's invitation.'

'Why not, your grace?'

'There are many reasons,' the bishop answered. 'First of all, the religious fervour of Dejach Kassa is questionable . . .'

'That is utterly untrue,' Samuel interrupted the bishop. 'No man has greater faith in Christ than Dejach Kassa; no man has greater desire to reshape the Church than Dejach Kassa.'

'That may be so,' the bishop agreed, 'but just the same his attitude to the Church leaves much to be desired. I have been informed that one of the major reforms he wants to introduce, if crowned emperor, is to reorganise the Church. I believe this should be left to the Church authorities. Another reason for me not to accept Kassa's invitation at this time is that I came to Abyssinia through Dejach Wube, and not through Dejach Kassa. Therefore I should get the approval of Dejach Wube before I venture to go to Gondar. And thirdly, my mission to this country is to preach the word of God, not to play politics.'

'But don't you see the danger in your refusal to accept the invitation, your grace? Don't you realise that Dejach Kassa will have to resort to the Roman bishop?'

'He won't dare to do that! He is just bluffing.'

'I can swear on the golden cross in your hand, your grace, that Dejach Kassa will certainly dare to do that.'

'He must be a fool, in that case, because he himself does not realise the consequences of such an undesirable act.'

'You mean you will turn the people against him?'

'I shall personally lead them in revolt.'

'You do not yet know the power of Dejach Kassa, your grace; he is a superman. He will in no time subjugate the people by his sword if you do lead them into revolt. I repeat, your grace, that Kassa Hailu is a superman.'

Aba Selama knitted his brows in thought. No head of the Ethiopian Orthodox Church had been so gravely threatened by anyone before, not in the entire history of the Church.

'What reply shall I take with me, your grace?' Samuel asked after a while.

'Tell him, Samuel, that at present I am not fit to travel, but that I shall think the matter over in due time,' the bishop said. In a lower tone he added, 'I must also see Dejach Wube about this matter.'

22

The Battle of Debre Sege

Following Samuel's report on his mission to the north, Kassa had no alternative but to attack Dejach Wube. Consequently, followed by his innumerable army, he set out on his northward journey on a cold day in the season of the small rains. The air was saturated with dampness, and the sky was sooty with threatening clouds overhead.

The soldiers marched in silence, some thinking of their quiet, warm homes, of their beloved wives, and of their beloved children; others gloomily looking forward to the approaching engagement against Wube. By now they were all tired, tired of the incessant march as well as of the perpetual bloodshed. After each battle they fought they had expected a respite, but each battle bred, as it were, yet another battle, keeping them moving on to yet further bloodshed. The victories they had won in the past kept their morale high, but there was a limit and an end to everything. They wanted rest; they wanted peace; they wanted to go and rejoin their families and enjoy the warmth of home, and they wanted reward. But every time they craved for rest and peace, the war drums were beaten, and they found themselves marching to the battlefield.

'I wonder when this bloody thing will end,' an embittered foot-soldier remarked, talking to his fellow-warrior.

'The devil knows when it will come to an end. Perhaps never. At least, not before the country is united.'

'I am fed up with it. I declare to God I am fed up with it.'

'Who isn't? But we all hope that everything will work out for the best in the end.'

'I see no purpose in the whole affair.'

'There I don't agree with you, brother, for we do have a purpose.'

'You say we have a purpose? I have fought by Dejach Kassa's side since his early days of rebellion in Quara, and yet he has rewarded me with nothing. Absolutely nothing. Now tell me what purpose I am fighting for?'

'We are all fighting to put an end to the anarchic rule of the princes, Rasses and Dejazmaches. We are fighting to put an end to the corruption of the Church authorities. We are fighting to re-annex the lost territories, we are fighting . . .'

'Words, words, words, and yet more words. For how many years have we heard those words repeated again and again? And what have we accomplished? Unity? We are as far from it as when we chased out Menen's governor from the district of Quara.'

'Our task has only started, my friend. It has not come to an end.'

'And it will never come to an end. We may defeat Dejach Wube in the coming battle. But believe me, that will not be the last battle we fight before the so-called unification of the Empire. And all this bloodshed, all this risk to one's life is for nothing – for no reward whatsoever.'

'As far as the reward is concerned, I should advise you to approach Dejach Kassa through Gebreye or Ingida, to remind him of your long service. Perhaps Dejazmach does not know you in person to reward you with something.'

'You mean he might have forgotten me, now that I am only a drop of water in the ocean of his followers?'

'Not really that. He might not have known you at all in the first place.'

'Impossible!' the aggrieved soldier exclaimed. 'We were so few in number in those early days that everyone knew everyone else by name. If he fails to recognise me now it's because he has forgotten me.'

'Anyhow, the best thing for you to do is to approach him through those who are very close to him.'

'Perhaps you are right,' the dissatisfied soldier said. 'But all the same I want to see the end of this perpetual bloodshed. I don't like it any more.'

The embittered foot-soldier was not the only person to grumble about the incessant bloodshed. Many others expressed a similar discontent, feeling they were fighting for no immediate, tangible purpose except for the war booties.

On the day of the battle, when Wube's army in magnificent array came into view, a general wave of murmuring swept from the back to the front of Kassa's marching soldiers, a thing that had never happened before. Kassa, sensing the explosive new situation, and foreseeing doom if his men's morale was not revived, abruptly halted his black charger, turned round to face his men, his eyes burning with anger, and spoke: 'Are you afraid, soldiers? Are you afraid of that old bastard of an aristocrat perching on the mountainside like a bird of prey, never certain whether to stay or take flight at the distant smell of the hunter? Are you afraid, soldiers, after all the battles you have so gallantly fought and won? Say yes, and we shall go back the way we came.'

'We fight, we fight. We fight to the last man!' came the uproarious voice of the soldiers, their courage revived by the magic words of their master.

'In that case we shall proceed,' Kassa affirmed, his heart bursting with joy. 'And I promise you that after this battle there shall be peace, and that my name shall no longer be Dejach Kassa, but Tewodros II, king of kings of Ethiopia.'

At the same time as Kassa's men advanced, shouting their battle cries, the sky split open; the rain came pouring down, accompanied by flashes of lightning. These were followed by peals of thunder that echoed and reverberated in the mountain ranges of Semen.

The sound of the cannons mingling with the crash of thunder drove Kassa's men to the point of madness. In the face of the firing ranks they fought their way across the cannon line, some dropping dead on the way while others proceeded up the mountainside.

In a short while the mountainside turned crimson with human blood, flowing downstream together with the waters of the rain. Dejach Wube fell to the ground, wounded by a pistol shot. His men lifted him up quickly and rushed him away to a cave on the other side of the mountain, blood dripping from his wounded chest.

The fight continued until Kassa's men discovered the cave where Dejach Wube lay groaning, and after fierce fighting they made him a captive.

The battle came to an end at the same time as the rains stopped falling. Silence followed; a terrible, deadly silence. Kassa and his living warriors surveyed the cold, still bodies of their friends and foes heaped the one over the other, and at last started moving towards their camp.

23

The Deal with Aba Selama

The first thing Kassa Hailu did after the victorious battle against Dejach Wube at Debre Sege was to have Aba Selama brought to his camp. The bishop, who had been informed of the ill-fate of Dejach Wube and who had been greatly shaken as a result, wasted no time in coming. He was accompanied by Aba Tekle and a host of other Church dignitaries.

Kassa received the bishop in pomp, as befitted a man of Aba Selama's rank, and opened their talk by saying, 'I am relieved and happy, your grace, that this time you are in good health.'

His words sounded half in earnest and half ironical. The bishop turned as white as a sheet of paper when he grasped the ironical sense of Kassa's words. In a defensive tone he said: 'What is it that you want of me?'

Aba Selama was speaking in Arabic, and Dejach Kassa in Amharic. Kassa could speak Arabic moderately well, and so could have conversed directly with the bishop. But his patriotic feeling made him communicate with the bishop in Amharic through Samuel acting as interpreter.

'Don't you really know what I want of you, your grace?'

'I don't know exactly what you want of me, Dejazmach, but I can perhaps guess.'

'And you agree to do what I want you to do?'

'On one condition only.'

'Say what it is, your grace.'

'The condition is that you first chase out the Jesuit from this land.'

Kassa Hailu smiled triumphantly. He had played his game so well that he was on the verge of winning it. His 'flirtation' with Bishop Jacobis had been a tactic all the way along. He was not so naïve as to believe that the people, to whom the national religion and the fatherland meant one and the same thing, would accept him as emperor after he had been crowned by a Catholic bishop. As far as the people were concerned, Roman Catholicism was next to paganism. But Kassa had used Bishop Jacobis as a tool with which to twist Aba Selama to his side.

'Is that your only condition?' he now asked the bishop, 'or do you want me to drive out all the missionaries, Catholics as well as Protestants?'

'I don't mind about the others for the time being. But Bishop Jacobis is undesirable. He is a menace to the Orthodox Church, and the worst influence in the entire country. And so he must go.'

'If I do promise to chase out Bishop Jacobis, are you going to crown me the day I want you to?'

'The dismissal of the Jesuit is my only condition.'

'Agreed,' Kassa said.

The coronation took place shortly afterwards in Debre Sege, in the very church that Dejach Wube had had newly built for his own coronation. It was not ceremonious or showy. Only the essentials were performed. What was important was that Kassa was finally crowned. The prediction had come true.

And the event released of course a new wave of gossip, and controversial arguments:

'How could he dare do it?' a respectable lady of the upper class remarked when she heard of the historical event. 'How could he dare put on his head the crown that once adorned the heads of the descendants of King David and King Solomon? How could he dare even touch it with his commoner's head?'

'They say that he, too, is a descendant of King David and of King Solomon,' another woman responded.

'Outrageous. That is most outrageous. It is a fabrication of liars and hypocrites. I tell you there isn't half a drop of royal blood in his veins.'

'But madam, they have traced his family tree, and they have discovered that in some distant past his ancestors were noble men, and royal blood flowed in their veins.'

'You believe that?'

'I have no reason not to believe it, madam.'

'Well, I tell you it is untrue. Kassa is an impostor. He is a disgrace to the nobility, a blemish on their unsullied ranks.'

'Madam, you had better watch your words, even if what you say is true.'

'Are you afraid of the impostor?'

'Impostor or not, he is a powerful man, madam. He is the Emperor.'

'Bah! He is a fake.'

'He has the power to cut out anyone's tongue, madam, including yours; you had better watch your words.'

'Any cut-throat has that much power.'

'Why don't you accept what other people accept, madam? They have suddenly discovered that he is of royal blood. And you must discover it as all the others have done.'

'Not me, my dear. I still have some self-respect left in me. I shall not accept a lie as though it were true. The son of a kosso-seller cannot have royal blood in his veins. It is scandalous even to suggest it.'

'But there is an explanation for it, madam.'

'What explanation are you talking about? We know the facts.'

'When he was poor and obscure, madam, no one took the trouble to trace his family tree. But when he started to become somebody many people started to dig for his roots. And now it is suddenly revealed to us that he is the descendant of King David and King Solomon.'

'Stop this nonsense, my friend, otherwise I shall have nothing to do with you any more. It is a disgrace to all decent people who have any respect for themselves. A commoner cannot become a nobleman overnight. And we all know the story of this man.'

'Believe it, all the same, madam; believe it for your own security. What is important is not always the truth as much as one's own safety.'

'I am an old woman, my friend, and I am not afraid of speaking the truth.'

The high-born lady wouldn't have it. Whatever others might believe, she was adamant in clinging to her view that Kassa was a commoner, not a member of the selected few. She was, however, curious, like everyone else, to see him the day he was to give a speech in Gondar. She was eager to see just what such an impostor looked like.

24

The Emperor Speaks

The royal drums started to rattle at dawn when the sky was grey, grey like ash. They rattled until the sky turned scarlet red; they continued to rattle until long after sunrise, until the last man in Gondar arrived at the place of calling. This was the day the emperor was to make a speech.

Like the Biblical shepherds who were guided by the twinkling stars to the manger so were the inhabitants of Gondar led by the rattling drums to the royal castles. They came in twos and threes and fours and flooded the open space that was the foreground of Atse Facil castle.

The emperor – attended by the empress, the bishop, Ingida, Gebreye, Gelmo and other dignitaries, including John Bell and Walter Chichile Plowden, the British envoy who had lately arrived from Massawa – stood on the balcony of the famous castle and looked down upon the crowd. They saw heads, and only heads; bare heads with black kinky hair and bald heads with no hair on them; heads with brown bushy hair; heads with hairs tressed and untressed; heads with white turbans, and green turbans, and black and white turbans.

Since daybreak, since the royal drums had started beating and rending the air with their vibrations, the people had come streaming into the royal enclosure. They pushed and pulled and jostled and nudged each others' sides and stepped on each others' toes in an effort to be a little closer to the castle, to see the face of the emperor and hear his new proclamation.

'Everyone must return to his fathers' profession,' the emperor pronounced. 'The farmer to his plough, the trader to his trade. I shall have no mercy on idlers and disturbers of the peace. Those who have no land may come and see me about it, and they shall get land. And those who have no oxen may come and see me too, and they shall get oxen. But woe to robbers and highway cut-throats, woe to idlers and disturbers of the peace, for I shall have no mercy on them.'

This was the substance of the emperor's speech when the chaff, the straw and all the other unnecessary materials were winnowed out of it. It was short, however, even in its entirety. A man of action rarely speaks at length. It was short and yet it was to the point. It heralded peace, encouraged work and condemned unlawfulness.

The crowd was pleased to hear the emperor's words, but few could believe that there was a possibility of peace or that the shiftas would return from the jungle to lead normal lives or that there would be no more rebellion in the land. How was that possible? Were there not other ambitious Kassas, other Goshus and Berus, and other Wubes to rise up in arms, either to break away from the grip of the central government and to declare their independence or on some pretext to overthrow Kassa Hailu and establish a new government in Gondar?

With doubt, with great uncertainty of the emperor's words the crowd dispersed to talk among themselves about the emperor's speech, about his rise to power and about his personality. He had once been a shifta himself, a highway robber, and now he condemned highway robbers. He had once been a rebel, and now he condemned rebels. What sort of a man was Kassa indeed? Many people could not answer that question, least of all Aba Tekle, who was among the throng that came to listen to the emperor's speech.

Aba Tekle had been following Aba Selama since the fall of Ras Ali, uncertain of the fate of the Church after the rebels assumed power. He followed Aba Selama to Debre Sege, and he followed him to Gondar after Kassa's coronation. Now that the bishop was somewhat reconciled with Kassa, Aba Tekle was more or less assured that Church affairs in Quara would go on as peacefully as before, and he was ready to go back to his parish. But he wanted to gather more information about the effects of the speech, about new appointments and other related matters.

When Aba Tekle returned to Quara a few days later, after collecting all the information he wanted, the first man he visited was Mulatu, his old-time friend, and one of the most devoted of the faithful of the district. Mulatu on his part had been impatiently waiting for the priest to arrive and tell him tales of Gondar. Crippled as he was, Mulatu learnt about what was going on in the country only through the eyes of others, especially through his neighbour, a Moslem trader, who usually travelled to Massawa twice a year and came back with as much news as goods; and through Aba Tekle, who met several people in Quara district and elsewhere and unfailingly, every week, fed him with news while Mulatu's wife fed him with Sunday delicacies. After the usual ceremony to drive out evil spirits from Mulatu's home, Aba Tekle took a seat, relaxed for a while and said to Mulatu: 'I come to you with good news.'

'Have you met him, Aba, have you met our Gebreye?' Aberash cut in before Mulatu could respond.

'Of course I have, though only for a brief moment.'

'Why don't you give Aba a chance to tell us about Gondar as a whole, Aberash? You have only your son in mind,' Mulatu admonished his wife.

'How about yourself, father of Gebreye? Isn't it about our son you want Aba to tell us first?'

'Let him tell us what he wants the way he wants to, and in the order he wants to.'

'Well, I meant to tell you both about Gebreye first,' Aba Tekle said. 'Gebreye has become a Fitawrari.'

'A what?' Aberash got excited without, however, understanding exactly what a Fitawrari was.

'He has become a Fitawrari,' Aba Tekle repeated.

'What does that mean, Aba? Oh, unfortunate that I am, when am I going to be knowledgeable?'

'A Fitawrari means exactly what it says, that is, one who leads in battle, Aberash. And Gebreye has become a Fitawrari, second in command of the Imperial Force – second only to Kassa himself.'

'But that must be dangerous, Aba. I thought they would make him something better than that.' There was concern in her voice.

'It's a great title, Aberash. You should be proud of your son.'

'I have always been proud of him. And I will always be proud of him,' she said, and trotted away to her guada to prepare the meal without listening to the rest of the news. Like any loving mother she was concerned mostly about her son. All the rest was secondary.

'What other news, Aba? Any other appointments?' Mulatu asked the priest.

'By the dozen, of course. A certain Ingida has become Ras and a certain Gelmo governor of Chilga district, responsible for the state prison in Sar Amba where they have confined the queen, and all the previous big officials. But I don't know whether you are familiar with these names.'

'Gebreye mentioned some of them to me when he came home

146

last time,' Mulatu said, and asked him of his impressions of the emperor in general.

'The emperor is an enigma to me, as he is to everyone else. I even feel uncomfortable to talk of him as the emperor. It sounds more natural to talk of him as Kassa, or as the rebel leader.'

'Call him what you want, but tell me your impressions of him.'

'I told you that he is an enigma to me, and a very unpredictable person. And to make clear what I mean by that I will tell you an incident that happened after his coronation speech in Gondar. Or have you already heard about it?'

'I have heard neither about Gondar, nor about any incident after the coronation speech.'

'Well, a group of robbers came to see the emperor after his speech, and – either trying to pick a flaw in his speech or in earnest – they said to him: "Your majesty, you proclaimed that everyone should go back to the profession of their fathers, the farmer to the plough, and the trader to his trade. But our fathers were bandits, your majesty, and like our fathers we, too, are bandits. We, therefore, ask your permission, your majesty, to let us practise our trade, and the trade of our fathers."

' "I cannot permit you to do such a thing," the emperor told the robbers. "If you have no land of your own I shall give you land to cultivate, and oxen, too, to make your work easier. But I cannot permit you to remain bandits, even if banditry was the profession of your fathers."

' "But we know no other work, your majesty. We don't know when to sow the seeds or when to harvest the crop," they said. "We don't know how to pull out weeds, or how to plough the field. Permit us, therefore, to practise our profession and the profession of our fathers."

' "Do I understand you to mean that you are not interested in anything except highway robbery?" the emperor asked them.

' "Not only are we not interested, your majesty; we know no other work," they said.

' "Well, well," the emperor said, and asked the spokesman of the bandits whether all the members of his group were present.

' "We could not all come at once, your majesty," the spokesman said. "Some stayed behind to secure food for us."

' "I see," the emperor replied. "In that case you will all come together tomorrow morning – all of you, I repeat – and in the meantime I shall see what can be done for you."

'The robbers returned the next morning. All of them. And they were many in number. Eighty, perhaps, or a little more. And the emperor asked them whether they still persisted in their request. They said yes. And can you guess, Ato Mulatu, what happened next?'

'I certainly wouldn't imagine that the emperor allowed the robbers to remain at large.'

'I say the emperor is a very unpredictable man, Ato Mulatu; what he did, in fact, in this particular case, was to give order to his soldiers to line up the robbers and shoot them down one by one like rabbits.'

'Really?'

'Yes, Ato Mulatu. They were executed one by one under my own eyes.'

'He does mean business, then?'

'No doubt, Ato Mulatu. There is no doubt he means business.'

At this juncture Aberash emerged from the guada carrying in her hands the hand-woven, colourful messob. She placed the messob before them, and they all started to munch the food in silence, their heads full of questions. They all wondered whether there was going to be a lasting peace in the land from now on, or whether the celebrations at Gondar marked only a period of truce.

Was there indeed going to be a lasting peace? Were there going to be no more shiftas? Were there going to be no more rebels? No other Kassas, Ingidas, Gelmos, Gebreyes? No other Menens, Alis, Wondirads, Bezabehs, Berus, Goshus or Wubes?

Only time could tell. Only time could testify.

Amharic words used in the text, and their meanings

Ferengi – white man (a corruption of the word 'French').

Gugse – a game played by men on horseback. (A mock-battle.)

Enjera – Ethiopian staple food. It is made from tiny grains called tef. Enjera is circular in shape, flat and honey-combed.

Guada – the storage section of a hut.

Messafint – aristocrats by blood.

Ras – a very high title (literally it means 'head').

Dejazmach – a high title (below Ras).

Wancha – a utensil wide at the mouth and narrow at the bottom, used for drinking-water, tella, etc.

Messob – a colourfully designed container out of which people eat traditional food. It is a symbol of the family.

Tella – local beer brewed by village women.

Shifta – a highway robber.

Kegnazmach – a title (below Fitawrari).

Medeb – the raised part of a floor near the wall, used for sleeping on like a bed.

Gembo – a clay jar.

Wanza – a tree with broad leaves and a thick trunk at maturity. It is used for making various types of traditional furniture.

Negarit – a drum.

Ato – Mr.

Fitawrari – a title (below Dejazmach and above Kegnazmach).

P3